Richard Gordon was born in 19 [on] to work as an anaesthetist at St Bartholomew's Hospital, and then as a ship's surgeon. As obituary-writer for the *British Medical Journal*, he was inspired to take up writing full-time and he left medical practice in 1952 to embark on his 'Doctor' series. This proved incredibly successful and was subsequently adapted into a long-running television series.

Richard Gordon has produced numerous novels and writings all characterised by his comic tone and remarkable powers of observation. His *Great Medical Mysteries* and *Great Medical Discoveries* concern the stranger aspects of the medical profession whilst his *The Private Life of...* series takes a deeper look at individual figures within their specific medical and historical setting. Although an incredibly versatile writer, he will, however, probably always be best known for his creation of the hilarious 'Doctor' series.

Doctor Gordon's Casebook

Richard Gordon

HOUSE OF
STRATUS

This edition published in 2001 by House of Stratus, an imprint of
Stratus Holdings plc, 24c Old Burlington Street, London, W1X 1RL, UK.

www.houseofstratus.com

Typeset, printed and bound by House of Stratus.

A catalogue record for this book is available from the British Library.

ISBN 1-84232-517-5

For, if a doctor's life may not be a divine vocation, then no life is a vocation, and nothing is divine.

STEPHEN PAGET

JANUARY

1 JANUARY

This year I shall keep a diary. Surely the reflections of a busy GP will be as valuable for future scholars as other hand mirrors held to history?

The doctor trespasses into the lives and thoughts of his patients deeper than Parson Woodforde into those of his parishioners, Fanny Burney those of the Georgian *beau monde* or Mr Pooter those of Gowing and Cummings. As Jean-Paul Sartre perceived, doctors know men as thoroughly as if they had made them.

My only problem is a style to dress yesterday's memories roused each morning with the discipline of a bugle-call. Like Pepys, 'Up betimes and to the surgerie, dispatched many vexatious patients with sundrie draughts, which methinks doth acte onlie on the minde...' Or like Gilbert White, 'The inhabitants enjoy a good share of health and longevity; and the parish swarms with children, mostly maladjusted.' Future scholars may find as instructive as Selborne my Kent market town of Churchford, seen for a quarter of a century through the wise and compassionate eyes of a dutiful journeyman doctor.

Unfortunately, I have such an appalling hangover after New Year's Eve on my friend the major's single malt, I shall defer my first entry till tomorrow.

8 JANUARY

I must make a second entry, to inform future scholars that I haven't had a hangover for a week.

RICHARD GORDON

10 JANUARY

I really *must* keep up this diary. I am haunted by the crass idiocy of my son
Andy, a mere house-surgeon at ancient St Botolph's Hospital in London,
where I am unashamedly proud that he followed me. He arrived home
this Sunday afternoon in a brand-new scarlet Alfa Romeo sports car,
which he is buying on HP. When I observed that in *my* houseman days we
were lucky to own a second-hand Morris Oxford, he replied flippantly,
'You lot weren't sharp enough to do the old Arthur Scargill act on the
bosses for a living wage among junior doctors. Clocking 120 hours a week
makes the old Umties' – he meant Units of Medical Time – 'tick up like a
taxi in a traffic-jam. Now I'm into geriatrics and cremation fees,' he ended
with relish, 'the ash-cash alone can buy a fortnight with a bird in
Marbella.'

When I expressed sadness at such venality, more expected of the
dockers than the doctors, he assured me cheerfully, 'Come off it, Dad,
medicine is far too difficult to be complicated by idealism.' He seems
happy, but a man who is not happy as a hospital houseman never will be.

11 JANUARY

I shall divorce my wife. She burst into morning surgery between patients
in a state of excitement because the washing-machine programme was
stuck and it was giving a continuous performance. A man exercising his
profession at home, within the sound of his children squabbling and the
smell of his lunch cooking, must be quarantined from domestic ills.

I demanded if Rembrandt, Beethoven or Leonardo da Vinci would be
dragged from their work by a leaky washtub. She responded that I groused
intolerably about washing-machine repairs costing more than Harley
Street consultations, and that Leonardo would certainly make a better job
of do-it-yourself than I did. We had macaroni cheese for lunch, which I
detest, and accused Sandra (wife) of using it to get her own back. She
replied tartly that it was cooked long before I was so rude. I have no
knowledge of such things, so could not retaliate, which put me in a worse
temper.

In the afternoon, to the public library (*Doctor on Call* label invaluable for parking). Unlike most medical people, who read nothing but *BMJ* (probably only the obituaries) and either *Amateur Gardening* or the *Yachting World* (depending on whether GPs or consultants), I retain contact with culture, if but a toehold. Find in 'Philosophy and Religion' Freud's *Wit and its Relation to the Unconscious*, will be fascinating to the Englishman enjoying national sense of humour.

Book stamped by Miss Fludde, my patient, a solemn, pale, dark-haired, large-eyed girl, suffering from mammary hyperplasia, what the laity call big tits. She, much concerned these are abnormal, and from cynosure of every eye in bus, supermarket, Torremolinos, etc., has recently enquired at surgery if whittling operation possible. Gave reassurance that what seemed to owners as obvious as dome of St Paul's is really as unnoticeable to passers-by as the lamp-posts. Advised against belittling Nature's bounty, many women as dead envious of it as of the Princess of Wales, must complain of skimpy endowment, have operations with silicone bags, can go wrong, embarrassing case of striptease artist developing starboard flat tyre during act.

Miss Fludde said she sensitive to young men regarding them through sweater as did ravening Tantalus the fruit-laden boughs forever swaying from his grasp (being well read), wishes to be loved for personality and intellect. Luckily suffering also from sprained knee, could dismiss her to the General for course of physiotherapy, which should temporarily take her mind off the tits.

Take book, tactfully averting eyes from relevant organs, though difficult.

13 JANUARY

Our daughter Jilly is a preclinical (bodies, biochemistry, bugs) student at St Botolph's, where I am ridiculously proud that she has followed me. Being Wednesday afternoon (traditionally free for games, study in library) she appeared on her Honda. Churchford convenient for London, was a country town when Mr Pickwick and Mr Winkle cavorted through Kentish lanes, but now inhabited mostly by executives, graded by expense of obligatory document-case on platform in morning, leaving their ladies all day to clean house, tend garden, play bridge, slim, have lovers, grow neurotic.

I like to interest Jilly in clinical medicine by relating my simpler cases. Like failure of the sympathetic nerves in the neck, Turner's syndrome. She laughed, 'Daddy, that's *Horner's* syndrome. Turner's is a sex chromosome anomaly, non-disjunction of the X, if you must know.' I reminded her that *I* had been qualified so long that I could remember prescriptions in Latin, a language which the patients could not understand, no more than the doctors. We had a warm argument, ending with her slamming the door, like the day she brought an Italian dentist home from Rimini.

Searched for Price's textbook of medicine to confront her in black and white, unfortunately discovered she was correct. I do so muddle names these days. I cannot even remember if Brearley or Botham is still captaining England.

Decided on *amende honorable* over tea and biscuit, but she snapped, 'Don't go on about it, I didn't come home for a viva.' She exclaimed a few seconds later, hadn't I noticed anything different about her? Am lost, she with same hair, scruffy jeans, etc. Jilly burst out, she is engaged to an accountant called Terence. I protested no physical sign of this condition, such as diamond ring, she responded no time yet to choose one, they met only at the Student Union Ball last Saturday. Jilly left for London digs as soon as wife returned from Friends of the General meeting, Jilly irritatingly disgruntled, though suspect less from non-appreciation of enhanced status than from bringing week's washing on back of Honda for Mum and finding the machine on the blink.

Anxiously discussed Terence with Sandra, age, colour of hair, colour of skin, etc. Sandra says an accountant OK, they treat other people's money with skilled detachment as I their diseases, grow wonderfully rich.

Settling with single malt before evening meal when Windrush at the General, who like all pathologists has a tediously juvenile sense of humour, telephoned with complicated joke about the colour, consistency and chemistry of mid-stream specimen I'd left at his lab. Apparently, hastily handed-in screw-top jar was wife's home-made lemon curd, intended for church bring-and-buy. Wonder what purchaser made of similar pot originating from bank manager.

24 JANUARY

Sunday. 10 a.m., still in bed. Bright, cold, Cambridge blue day. Heard Sandra busily bumping round house. All alone. Andy on call, Jilly presumably on passionate weekend with Terence. Reread colour supplement.

'Richard!' Sandra entered, shocked. 'Don't forget we're going for Sunday morning drinks to those awful new patients with the Rolls.'

'I'm ill.'

Tender concern. 'You poor darling! What's the matter?'

'Brain tumour. Trigeminal neuralgia. Cranial arteritis. I'm not certain.'

'How can you continually scoff at your patients' medical myths,' she continued severely, 'when persisting in believing, after an evening at the Hatchetts' (professional colleague) 'that single malt whisky never gives anyone a hangover?'

I rose, to seek aspirin in medicine cupboard in bathroom. This a converted dressing-room and freezing. We live in redbrick Victorian house with every modern inconvenience. Exclaimed, 'God! How did we manage to collect all those bottles with peculiar coloured stuff running down the outside? All those pitifully deformed tubes? These little brown containers, showered by the government on its lucky sick like confetti? It looks like an arsenal for chemical warfare. What's this mixture, ΣΙΡΟΗΙΟΝ ΑΓ ΕΝΗΛ ΚΑΣ? It seems you have to ΛΕΓΠΕΡΙΕΧΕΙ ΣΟΧΟΡΣΖΘΓ with it.'

'Surely you remember, dear? You developed d & v in Rhodes four summers ago.'

'Oh, yes! That funny little chemist's beside the retsina shop...our first holiday unbothered with the children since our honeymoon. There seems enough athlete's foot powder here for the entire Olympic team,' I noticed. 'And why all these oils and ointments for bunions and callosities?'

'Have you forgotten that enormous Dutch au pair who grew so hysterical about her feet?'

'Of course! Always – as I used to say – in tears amid the alien corn-cure. Wasn't that fifteen years ago? How time flies. Vitamin tablets! Quite disgraceful. No normal person needs vitamin tablets.'

She took the little drum tenderly. 'I swallowed those when I was pregnant with Andy.'

'So you did dear,' I remembered. 'Twenty years in the past. And you've hardly changed.'

'Nor you, Richard,' she responded touchingly, 'apart from no longer needing this bottle of hair conditioner. Oh, look! Jilly's Mary-had-a-little-lamb medicine glass, when we had drachms and scruples like £sd.'

'Medicine went metric with far less fuss than the grocery trade.'

'These yellow capsules…'

I seized them. 'They shouldn't be in the cupboard at all.' I could not suppress a gulp. 'Poor James was taking them when he died.'

'Oh! So he was…only three, the little dear.'

'You know, I still blame myself for his death. It's a hard thing to say, but I didn't diagnose his infection early enough, I didn't take him to someone who knew more about it than I did.'

'You mustn't suffer remorse about it for the rest of your life, darling.'

'Yes,' I agreed. 'I suppose it's a good twelve years now since James started barking and wagging his tail in Heaven. What's this? "To pep up your rechsteineria Leucotricha." I know my anatomy's a bit weak, but where is it?'

'In a pot in the living-room.'

'Now, these things like green Smarties are the remains of that double-blind trial for the university, using doctors as guinea-pigs. It should be enormously reassuring for the public, the care we take testing new drugs. Not only the patient, but the physician, doesn't know whether the identical tablets are real or only placebos.'

'But you knew that every month's course they sent you were placebos.'

'Yes, it soon got round the profession that the placebos floated when you chucked the lot down the loo. Look! My old jockstrap. Sad. Moths. Who needed these tranquillizers?'

'I did, dear,' Sandra told me crisply. 'During our crisis. When you nearly ran off with that twenty-year-old receptionist.'

'H'm. And I suppose this calamine was for the seven-year itch? Odd, you can tell the history of a marriage from its medicine cupboard. What's this? Drops for earwax?'

'When I nearly left *you*, because you never seemed to listen to a word I said.'

I read on a pink label, *Comprimés pour les Névralgies, Migraines, Grippes, Courbatures Fébriles.*

'We can chuck *this* old tube out.'

She snatched it. 'No you don't! We brought it on our honeymoon at Cannes.'

'I hope you didn't have *all* those things?'

'Oh, no! Well, not all at once.'

'We've enough liquid paraffin here to move the bowels of the earth,' I discovered. I uncorked a corrugated blue bottle, sniffed and sneezed. 'This liniment's a bit strong.'

Sandra smelt it gingerly. 'For rubbing on Jilly's horses.'

A fond memory suffused me. 'Remember that wonderful P G Wodehouse story?' I asked. ' "Much has been written about the accident of birth" – the Master wrote – but had the Earl of Emsworth been born a horse he wouldn't have gone screaming round Blandings at midnight after treating his sprained leg.'

Sandra dropped her eyes. 'Do you know, Richard... I was laughing over that page on a dull night-duty when we first met at St Botolph's.'

'I can see you now, my sweet.' I replaced the liniment in the cupboard and kissed her.

'Richard! That was quite passionate.'

'I'm feeling passionate. It's either the memories, or something escaping from one of the bottles.'

'But it's breakfast time!'

'In France, it's the most popular hour for love. That's why they all gobble a quick croissant, instead of sitting down to bacon and eggs.'

'Oh, Richard, darling...' She snuggled against my pyjama buttons. The phone rang.

'Damn!' The telephone continually mars the intimacies of a medical household, and is recognized in the profession as a leading cause of coitus interruptus.

'I'll answer it,' said Sandra.

She generally did. It's as unproductive for a doctor to be exposed to the patient direct as it is for a politician to the voters on a phone-in.

I poked through the cupboard. Pink tablets, to be taken as directed. How mysterious. Were they an expectorant or a cough suppressive? To cheer you up or calm you down? Make you sleep or keep you awake? Sharpen your appetite or check your obesity? Grow hair or remove it? That's medicine, I reflected. The world is full of people who want children but can't have them, or have too many and can't stop, with noses and bosoms too big or too small, people who are attempting to live forever or attempting to commit suicide...

'It's those awful patients with the Rolls.' Sandra came from the bedroom. 'He's down with a headache, so wants you to come professionally instead of for drinks.'

'Splendid! They're private patients who, better still, pay cash on the nail, and perhaps' – I picked up the bottle – 'I can find out what these little pink pills *really* do.'

25 JANUARY

Harassing morning surgery, six women think themselves pregnant (two married). Always a lot of it about this time of year, owing to Christmas. Entered kitchen for lunch, found only washing-machine man, surrounded by washing machine like the entrails at an untidy post-mortem, leaning against the wall saying he felt queer.

Examined him in surgery, assured him nothing wrong. His only complaint tiredness, remarkable as he'd taken entire morning to anatomize machine. Also pins-and-needles in legs, which I told him everyone has, like itchy arse. A difficult patient, he slouched off, leaving mess.

26 JANUARY

Jilly telephoned, saying would love to bring Terence for a meal on Sunday evening. Instantly perturbed. Am unbothered finding self in presence of City wizards, royalty opening new wing of General, even headmasters, as know what all look like undressed. But with children's camp-followers must check tongue against slightest disparagement in or out of earshot, press hospitality, display solicitude for comfort, as possibility of their becoming in-laws, who are famous for remembering slights real or imagined for ever. Furthermore, sobering thought, pallid youth with dandruff and boils in polytechnic T-shirt, leather trousers and tennis shoes, if weds daughter, will be attending your own funeral.

Sandra more concerned about fare. Sunday roast out, as family like it well-cooked, I like it mooing. She decided on something straightforward to impress Terence we perfectly ordinary middle-class family with interest in medicine.

27 JANUARY

Where was I?

Yes! I recognized it now. The desk loaded with bric-a-brac, the classical prints, Egyptian fragments, framed fossils. The couch covered with the Turkish rug, on which I was lying, my head among generous pillows. It was No. 19 Bergasse, Vienna, over the butcher's shop.

'And you,' I asked the man with the white nanny-goat beard, horn-rimmed glasses and blue serge suit, 'must be Dr Freud?'

'Just say the first thing which comes into your head.' He sat heavily in the velvet armchair.

'I'm delighted to meet you, because I found in our public library a couple of weeks ago your *Wit and its Relation to the Unconscious*. I'm a wit buff – Frank Muir and Peter Ustinov on the telly, but it hasn't been invented yet, so you wouldn't know about it. Wit, I always say, lightens our drab world like a smile from a pretty girl or finding an unexpired parking meter. Even my friend the major gets pretty witty in the golf club, if you catch him between his fourth and sixth scotch-and-soda, after that he's straightforward ENSA 1944.'

'Just say the first thing which comes into your head.'

'I opened the 388 pages as eagerly as a bottle of Bollinger, but if I may be frank – and what apter place to be frank than a psychiatrist's couch? – it's about as entertaining a read as the phone book. Your first gagwriter is Heine, the one about the poor lottery agent boasting that Baron Rothschild treats him as an equal – quite FAMILLIONAIRE, in capitals.'

'Ho, ho, ho!' Freud held his sides. 'I told that over our *Apfelstrüdel* in the café Mozart to Jung and Krafft-Ebbing, they fell about.'

'Obviously it tickled you, Dr Freud, because you explain the joke from pages 15 to 22. Then you chortle about it all over again from pages 215 to 220.'

Freud rolled round his chair. 'When I told it again over *Leberwürst* in the *Bierkeller* to the Marquis de Sade and Leo von Sacher-Masoch, they laughed till it hurt.'

'Now your next quip…oh, dear. If you made it in an English pub, you'd be in dead trouble with the Race Equality Commission, the Council for Civil Liberties and probably the Friends of the Earth. About the two Jews meeting at the municipal bath-house – '

'Ach!' Freud dried his eyes with a bandanna. 'I gave that to Havelock Ellis and Adler in the *Kaffeehaus* over our *Sachertorte*, they pissed themselves.'

'Well, I mean, the first Jew asks, "Have you taken a bath?" And the other replies, "Is one missing?" Not exactly Oscar Wilde.'

Still shaking, Freud urged, 'Let me explain it.'

'Don't bother,' I said hastily. 'You *did* explain it, for the next twelve pages.'

Freud slapped his thigh. 'Then you must hear the mayonnaise joke.'

'No, no! *Not* the mayonnaise joke, *please*,' I implored. 'I expect when you were full of *Wienerschnitzel* and *Spälese* in the Prater with Nietzsche and Melanie Klein, the mayonnaise joke made Abraham Lincoln sound like Bob Hope. But *Der Witz* was published in Germany during 1905, when…well, Shaw was writing things like, "An Englishman thinks he is moral when he is only uncomfortable," and "Do not do unto others as you would they should do unto you. Their tastes may not be the same," and

"Home is the girl's prison and the woman's workhouse". And Saki was saying she was a good cook as cooks go, and as cooks go she went.'

Freud stared. 'I don't get it. Why is it funny that the cook should go, particularly if she was a good cook?'

'I suppose I *could* explain it like you do, Dr Freud, but it *is* rather like dissecting a butterfly with a pneumatic drill.'

Freud was on his knees by the couch. 'Don't you like the blacksmith joke? How they hanged the tailor for the smithy's crime, because there were two tailors in the village but only one blacksmith. *Please* say you like the blacksmith joke,' he wheedled. 'It's genuine Hungarian.'

'Dr Freud,' I returned sternly. 'I can no longer applaud the insubstantial pageant you made on such stuff as dreams.'

'But why?' He looked bewildered. 'Everyone knows that Freud and dreams are like Escoffier and sauce.'

'Because a man becomes discredited *totally* in the eyes of any Englishman who suspects he has no sense of humour. Look at Richard III and Mr Heath.'

'But I *have* a sense of humour. That is obvious. I wrote a book about it.'

'To be just – and our English fair play is, of course, as famous as our humour – a few nuggets pan from the Danubian gravel. On page 204 you remark that "wit overcomes the inhibitions of shame and decorum" in females. This in England is known as chatting up the birds. You declare that wit can overthrow judgement, shatter respect for institutions, even for truth itself. What a terrible weapon, if ever one of our politicians got his hands on it. And how I agree with you, wit is awfully useful for being rude. An Englishman prefers to swallow the vilest insult rather than risk appearing a poor sport. That wit is unrelated to intelligence, that wits have "a predisposition to nervous affections", every literary and theatrical agent must know from Shaftesbury Avenue to Sunset Boulevard. You decide that wit is "an impulse comparable to the impulse toward sexual exhibition". Well, it's better to sparkle than to flash. What is truth? said jesting Pilate. What is wit? asked sober-sided Freud. I'll tell you. It's pulling the rug of reality from under an idea's feet.'

He leapt up. '*Himmel!* I have it. You English possess absolutely no sense of humour. How can you, when you don't take jokes seriously?'

11

'That's a worse insult than telling Frenchmen they can't cook, Italians they're impotent or the Russians that they actually like Communism.'

'Roll over! I am going to administer psychotherapy.'

With a wild laugh, he punched me in the ribs.

'Richard, wake up!' commanded Sandra. 'You're making a noise like the giant panda on heat.'

'Eh? What? I was dreaming of having a consultation with Sigmund Freud.'

'Coals to Newcastle, isn't it?'

'That wasn't very witty.'

'Really? I *am* sorry. If you want wit at four-thirty a.m., you'd better go and sleep with Pamela Stephenson. Good night.'

28 JANUARY

Horrified at a letter from a practitioner I'd never heard of, saying he'd a serious ethical complaint concerning Mr Tarwitch, whom I'd also never heard of, but is apparently the washing-machine man. He consulted his own doctor with insulting speed, who diagnosed Guillain-Barré syndrome (politically fashionable), put him off work for six months, and is threatening me with disciplinary action in the General Medical Council and a malpractice suit in the courts. Bloody sure the patient's a malingerer and the doctor's a paranoic. Probably in cahoots, appalling that professional rectitude today attracts only blackmail, and patients are less grateful for a free consultation than a free haircut. Threw letter in the fire, instantly regretted it, as sneaking suspicion they may have a case.

Account came for repair of washing machine, you could get a minor operation at the Princess Grace for it.

30 JANUARY

Absurdly worried what Terence will make of us tomorrow. Medical households always in the newspapers, doctors working 18-hour day, comes home at night energy-depleted, emotionally anaemic, 3000 of us alcoholics (of which 10% cirrhotic). Wives suffer worse, feel as neglected as the first Mrs Rochester in *Jane Eyre*, take to drink, drugs, lovers, the lovers preferable as non-toxic. Decide am over-sensitive, Terence will happily find us a normal, friendly, cultured family.

Andy arrived after lunch, in Alfa Romeo naturally. When I repeated lecture on extravagance, he laughed, 'Dad, this motor draws birds faster than battery-farm machinery.' Invited me to drive. Must confess, nippy little job, more fun dodging around the juggernauts than my four-year-old four-door, started to imagine getting one, but remembered Chris (in advertising) and his male menopause, he bought Ferrari, Sidi clothes, Cellini after-shave, dark glasses, Via Veneto haircut, probably lived on pasta, embarrassing at golf club, particularly as the major after monthly dinners tends to relive Anzio.

31 JANUARY

Gin and ton with Toby (Dr Hatchett) in golf club this evening. Coming home to join family encountered car smash. Usually don't stop, firemen far more practical than GPs, also patients sometimes behave like Mr Tarwitch, if survive. But pulled up, attended bystanders cut with glass, fainting, etc., driver needed no treatment. Arrived home to find a green Metro at door, presumably Terence's, family just gone into dinner, are used to the profession transforming meals into Mad Hatter's tea parties.

'Daddy, this is Terence,' said Jilly.

'How *do* you do?' Shook hands heartily.

Terence pink, fair, curly, in accountant's suit, on best behaviour. 'So glad you can join our simple family dinner, Terence. Sorry I'm late, darling,' I apologized to Sandra. 'I stopped to lend a hand with an accident at the crossroads by the Blue Boar.'

'Anyone hurt?' Sandra served steaming platefuls.

'Only the driver. Had his head through the windscreen.'

'Did he sever the carotid, Daddy?' Jilly has her eye on the St Botolph's Anatomy Prize this summer, which would make me even prouder, as I always found anatomy incomprehensible.

'Oh, both of them,' I told her. 'And the jugulars and trachea. The oesophagus as well, probably. Doubtless he fractured his vertebrae, too. There was blood all over the bonnet.'

'Dead, Dad?' enquired Andy.

'As a doornail. Perfectly obvious, as soon as I pulled at the hair. Pretty well decapitated.'

'I heard about one on the M4 last week,' Andy recalled. 'The head was in the rear. Sort of backseat driver, you might say.'

I took my place at the table, sighing, 'No seat-belt, the stupid fellow. Why, steak and kidney pudding! I love steak and kidney pudding, a real treat you've occasioned, Terence.' I beamed at him. 'Would you pass the mustard?'

After some seconds' silence, July told her fiancé a shade sharply, 'You're staring at it.'

'Well, Terence, we have only one rule of family behaviour,' I continued warmly. '*Absolutely no shop at meals.* It makes a nice rest for Andy, who's a house-surgeon at St Botolph's. Such an excellent system in our hospitals,' I reflected, forking the deliciously soggy suet. 'The newly qualified houseman, you know, always works with the experienced consultant. The one is horrified by the awful limitations of his knowledge. The other is completely confident of knowing absolutely everything. That's the houseman.'

'Where do you *do* your accountancy, Terence?' Sandra leant towards him cordially.

'In the City, Mrs Gordon.' He seemed relieved to talk on his own subject. 'I've just started with Stallybrass, Turpin, Fishwick and Dolittle. They're a very respected firm, widely known in the business world.'

'*Fishwick*, did you say?' Andy demanded at once across the table. 'That your boss' name? What an amazing coincidence! He was hauled into St Botolph's last week from a City dinner.'

'That's right, Andy,' Terence told him. 'Mr Fishwick was at Moneychangers' Hall when he was struck. We were all very upset the next day in the office.'

St Botolph's in Citygate Lane acts as a clearing station for the casualties of commerce – coronaries, perforated ulcers, alcoholism, suicide, etc.

14

'But it was *my* surgical firm who cut him.' Andy glowed with interest. 'It was a perf, Dad. And what a specimen! The duodenum pretty well in two separate pieces.'

'Really?' I exclaimed. 'You usually only see that sort of thing in a bottle in the path lab.'

'He was jolly lucky that Old Rolly-Poly happened to be the carver,' continued Andy.

'That's Sir Rollo Basingstoke,' Jilly explained, smiling.

'Oh, yes,' Terence said. He seemed a refreshingly quiet young man. 'We were relieved to hear in the office that one of London's most distinguished surgeons – '

Andy chuckled. 'In the middle of the operation, with Rolly-Poly's hands deep in the abdomen, he said, "Crikey! I wouldn't use this chap's guts for garters, my socks would fall off." Dreadful mess to clear up in the peritoneal cavity, it was like a kitchen sink.'

I reminisced – how pleasant with one's own son! – 'When *I* was a young houseman, we always seemed to be mopping out diced carrots and beer from those endless gurgling coils of intestine.'

'Not now, the affluent society has reached the very extremes of our anatomy, it's more likely to be scampi and rosé. Your boss really had been doing himself well,' Andy enlightened Terence. 'The theatre sucker-bottle absolutely reeked of garlic.'

'Your steak and kidney all right, Terence?' Sandra asked with concern.

'I'm…I'm a very light eater, Mrs Gordon.'

'Hi – !' Jilly stared curiously at the tip of her raised fork. 'Look at this, my kidney distinctly shows the calyces and pelvis. That's where the cholesterol stones are formed, isn't it?'

'Except, Jilly,' her brother replied airily, 'that kidney stones are urates.'

'No, they're not,' she corrected him sharply. All medical women know their minds as well as they think they know other people's. 'I ought to know. We're doing stones in pathology.'

'Perhaps you are. But I'm qualified and you're not,' Andy returned crushingly. 'You're mixing them up with gallstones.'

'I am not!'

'Yes, you *are*!'

'Not!'

'Are!'

'Children, children,' Sandra interrupted mildly. 'You haven't improved since you used to squabble over the bathwater. And do remember what Daddy said – *no shop*.'

'Terence will think we're quite as quarrelsome a family as the Lears.' I smiled at him. Jilly had gone pink. Medical women take slights upon their knowledge as sorely as actresses upon their looks.

'I say, Dad, where's the booze?' enquired Andy with his customary directness.

Apologizing, I crossed to the sideboard. Sandra mentioned, while helping herself to more sprouts, 'Funny how things come back to you. When I was nursing at St Botolph's, the professor suddenly went mad on kidney research. Wanted twenty-hour specimens from the whole ward. Twenty-four hours, imagine! That's an awful lot of urine, there were bottles of it all over the place, you could hardly move.'

I smelt the cork approvingly. 'This hock is beyond the pocket of a mere GP, Terence, I'm sure you'll like it. A present from the wine-shipper himself. Well, his widow. He died last month, cirrhosis of course.'

'Daddy, what's the basic pathology of cirrhosis?'

'The liver goes tawny, Jilly. Thickening and hardening, with knobs all over. The "hobnail liver", they used to call it, plenty of post-mortem specimens bottled in your pathology lab.'

'I...er, think I'll just have a glass of water, Dr Gordon.'

Alarmed silence at a prospective teetotal son-in-law was broken by Sandra directing, 'Andy, be a dear and get a bottle of Perrier from the fridge, but don't disturb Daddy's pus specimens for the path lab at the General tomorrow.'

'Ok, Mum. What bugs, Dad?'

'Streptococci, staphylococci, there's an odd outbreak of boils.' I poured myself a brimming glass of *Rheingau*, there being one share less. 'People seem to be getting them all over, neck, buttocks, scrotum.'

'*Eau-la-la*, Terence, as they say in the adverts.' Andy reappeared from the kitchen. 'Talking of the St Botolph's path lab, there wasn't much of this stuff drunk at the party for the brand-new one. Oh, it's the post-mortem Hilton, every convenience, comfortable room for a hundred stiffs, luxuriously fitted drawers –'

I interrupted with a laugh. 'Did I ever tell you, Andy? When I was a houseman, I once pulled a drawer where the ratchet thing had bust, the corpse went flying across the PM room and hit the professor of morbid anatomy in the umbilicus.'

'God! How funny!' Andy upended the bottle.

'I…er, Jilly,' Terence said, 'I think I must go to the toilet.'

'But Terence, you only just went. I hope you haven't got congenital hypoplasia of the bladder?' she suggested with a faint frown.

'You'll never believe this, Dad,' continued Andy, 'but the idiotic builders had connected the refrigeration and heating systems the wrong way, so the first load of corpses weren't frozen overnight, but stewed. You can't imagine the stink in the morning.'

To our surprise, Terence jumped up from the table. 'Heavens! Is that the time? I must go. At once. I'm sorry, Mrs Gordon…Jilly…but tomorrow I'm doing the audit for the Massive Concrete Co., and I need a good night's sleep.'

'But don't you want to use the lav first?' Jilly called, he already moving briskly to the door.

'No. No time. I need a lot of sleep. Goodbye. Charming evening. So enjoyed it. Don't see me out.'

'Well!' exclaimed Sandra. The Metro instantly accelerated off. 'Surely he could have kept an eye on his watch, if he had to be early to bed?'

'What odd young men you bring home, Jilly,' I observed.

'Yes, Daddy. I don't think I liked him very much, anyway. He had no conversation.'

'Seconds?' asked Sandra.

'Please, Mummy. *Delicious* pud.'

FEBRUARY

1 FEBRUARY

Giving this diary up. Have overlooked the intimate lives of my patients. It is hard enough being an overworked GP, without getting up fifteen minutes early to write about it. Anyway, all diarists are frightful egotists. Pepys probably had personalized number plates on his sedan chair.

2 FEBRUARY

Must persist with my diary, to astound future scholars with the amazingly interesting cases to be found in a humdrum general practice, so long as the doctor is sharp-eyed, quick-witted, well informed and highly organized.

Mrs Paish, the manageress of our local launderette, appeared at morning surgery in a state. Last night she suffered a terrifying attack, burning chest and jaws, palpitations, copious weeping. I asked but one question – 'How was the chop suey?' She amazed, as if I Sherlock Holmes unmasking Hound of Baskervilles.

I smilingly explained what we doctors call the 'Chinese Restaurant Syndrome'. Alarming symptoms arise from a personal idiosyncrasy to the flavouring agent monosodium glutamate, added to Chinese food as liberally as Scotsmen combine whisky with haggis. Mrs Paish was vastly relieved, had already imagined herself on the Green Line to Harefield for a cardiac transplant. I reassured her it was all heredity, an 'inborn error of metabolism', no danger, no treatment. She thanked me touchingly, saying how lovely to have an understanding doctor, she personally never went along with the widespread notion of GPs surly sods never looking up from their prescription pads even when the patients were dying from Legionnaires' disease.

How more gratifying would practice be, were more patients as appreciative and courteous as Mrs Paish!

5 FEBRUARY

Snowing. Two or three coronaries may be expected from middle-aged executives shovelling their drives.

Down to surgery at 8.30 a.m. Smallish bright room, primrose paint, couch, instrument cupboard, one-eyed teddy for diverting children, net curtain, looks south over back garden – lawn, roses, rhodos, serves as Galen's (dog's) loo. Patients wait on mauve plastic chairs in Edwardian hall, marshalled by Mrs Shakespear (receptionist) in white coat, who enjoys local reputation as Cerberus, the three-headed dog guarding Hades, though she is tiny, dark and curly, with a turned-up nose and a husband in greetings cards.

My final patient was the major, who always craftily delays his appearance to minimize waiting and increase his chance of a cup of coffee.

I greeted him sociably across the consulting desk, 'The old back again? You really should wear a corset. The NHS provides a perfectly serviceable garment free of charge, would do you the world of good. You've just got to lose your association with frothy lace and long black suspenders reaching to your socks.'

'Doc, I've got a complaint.' He took the rush-bottomed patients' chair, sticking out his pepper-and-salt-clad legs. 'I woke in the middle of last night with a ghastly pain in my chest. Honestly, thought I was a goner. I dialled your number, got your answering-back machine. Eventually, some sprig turned up. He could have been the paperboy with a haircut, for all I knew. He cured me, certainly – told me to drink a glass of hot water and not to make such a fuss – but that's beside the point.'

'My dear Major, you were privileged,' I enlightened him. Instead of a fusty GP, you received treatment by some bright young doctor moonlighting from an exacting and educative hospital post. He didn't summon you to the surgery. No! He visited you in your own home, from sheer professional zeal. And because, unlike me, he gets paid extra for doing so.'

'But you know my carcass as well as you know the bunkers on the golf course,' the major objected. 'I don't care for strange hands being set on it.'

'You're not the first to complain about the doctors' deputizing service,' I admitted. (Chris had invited us last night to an advertising agents' ball in town, interesting affair, lavish, lush and lecherous. Naturally, rang the Hippocrates Answering Service first. They employ young doctors struggling to raise their professional status and a young family at the same time – difficult.) 'We're no longer prepared to be on call twenty-four hours a day, seven days a week.'

'Why not? That's a doctor's vocation.'

'Look, how would you like to stay cold sober twenty-four hours a day?'

'I'm beginning to follow the thread of your argument.'

'Patients in the know call the deputizing service at night deliberately. They want to check from a young specialist if their GP's talking rubbish. After all, they don't have to pay for the consultation. The GP does. I agree, a strange face in the consulting room over a week or two can unsettle the practice. When I took Sandra to Venice last autumn – '

'Good hols?'

'Holiday?' I was shocked. 'A busy and devoted GP can't take two holidays a year. That was study leave, paid by the Health Service, to attend an international meeting on the Pathophysiology of Pregnancy. Utterly fascinating subject, I assure you.' The weather was lovely, and I discovered the Bellini – a delightful mixture of champagne and peach juice. 'I then employed a diligent locum hailing from Shanka – a burstingly emergent nation in Africa.'

'Asia.'

'Really? What does it matter, these days of jet travel?'

'I remember the chappie. Like others of that ilk, his grip on English was as odd as a Mason's handshake. I told him I was always whacked on Friday nights.'

'He got interested?'

'He got bloody excited. Tried sending me to a psychiatrist.'

'Ah, dear! Colloquial English can cause more trouble in the consulting-room than in the classroom.'

I rummaged in the desk for a blue-covered pocket-sized book.

The major regarded it as suspiciously as a guide to quick money on the turf. '*A Manual of English for the Overseas Doctor?*'

'It's written by a lady at the British Council, crammed with useful information for my next locum.' I turned the pages. ' "How to address the Deputy Matron". Personally I'd avoid it. Did you know that *GP* can mean either *general practitioner* or *guinea-pig?* Reasonable, from the way the Ministry treats us. Now, the breasts. What do you suppose the English call them? "The bosom", "the buffers", "the top part", "the Charleys", that's got an asterisk – *Not commonly used in polite society*. Really? Perhaps ladies live a sheltered life on the British Council. Cockney, too. Your "jam tart" rhymes with cardiac trouble, and when you talk of "the twig and berries" you're referring to your asterisk. "I have a gastric stomach" seems a painful case of tautology.'

'At least, I won't have to indicate my back pain to your next equatorial locum by using a putter.'

'You will if he's an EEC doctor. No PLAB for them. They needn't speak English at all. It's in the Treaty of Rome. Land at Heathrow, a taxi to Hallam Street, pay the GMC seventy quid and start scrubbing up.'

The major snorted. 'Shouldn't like a fellow stinking of garlic, or making a din clicking his heels, when I was feeling under the weather.'

'I'm preparing for exactly that emergency.' I produced some sheets of lined foolscap. '*A Travellers Phrase Book for Use in the Home*. French is easy, just talk about *les rognons, le foie, les tripes*, they regard the body as an *à la carte* menu. Have you ever sent for a policeman or an ambulance in Italian when there's been an accident? It sounds absolutely lovely. You can sing it to the tune of "La Donna è Mobile" Listen –' I threw open my arms. '*Chiama una guardia...un'ambulanza...c'è stata una disgrazia –*'

'You've a remarkably fine voice, Doc,' he complimented me.

'I was renowned for it at St Botolph's, on a Saturday night.'

The major rose. 'See you for a prescription in the golf club at seven?'

'Sorry.'

'On call, I suppose? No paperboy to tend your patients?'

'No. I've got to watch the TV programme called…something like, "What Your Doctor Would Tell You If Only He Knew It Himself". Must keep up to date. I'm a conscientious GP, you see. Good morning.'

I enjoy a consultation with the major. I really don't think he takes me more solemnly than I do him.

8 FEBRUARY

Horrified to receive a letter from Middlewitch, Thorneycroft, Blews and Nutt (Solicitors) saying their client the Ho Ho Ho! Oriental Takeaway was suing me for slander. Apparently, that stupid bitch Mrs Paish went straight from the surgery to the Ho Ho Ho! Oriental Takeaway in Station Road and abused them like a fishwife, shouting from the street that I'd diagnosed they'd poisoned herself, husband and family. I wrote back instantly, saying that Mrs Paish's condition was an inborn error of metabolism, all genetic, the Ho Ho Ho! Oriental Takeaway no more responsible than for the colour of her eyes or the unfortunate appearance of her children.

I am disgusted at Tom Blews being party to this outrageous slur on my professional integrity, as I actually *put him up* for the golf club.

9 FEBRUARY

Appalling episode in morning surgery. Entire staff of Ho Ho Ho! Oriental Takeaway appeared, about twenty Chinamen, not in the slightest inscrutable, all very angry. It seems that Mrs Paish last night, after brooding on grievances, or probably pissed, appeared at the counter of Ho Ho Ho! Oriental Takeaway demanding money back, accompanied by friends and neighbours convinced they had suffered the same symptoms. (Patients are unbelievably suggestible, a TV programme on elephantiasis and everyone's got it, though probably friends and neighbours all pissed, too.)

Mrs Shakespear ashen-faced, worried the Chinamen were hiding under their anoraks those choppers which reduce an entire pig to diced pork in minutes. I faced them in surgery, feeling like General Gordon on the banks of the Yangtse in 1864, tried to reason that the Chinese

Restaurant Syndrome was a handy medical term like Christmas Disease (nothing to do with gluttony, named after first unfortunate patient). Does not sink in. Anyway, too much noise to expound even the difference between Peking and Bombay Duck.

Mrs Shakespear had meanwhile communicated her alarm outside to Miss Drage, waiting for consultation about anxiety neurosis. They resolved to dial 999, police car arrived, making a frightful din, the crew seemed to expect a scene like St Valentine's Day in Chicago, threatened the usual police tactic when frustrated of arresting everybody in sight, including myself. I explained patiently the Chinamen were only suffering a misapprehension about inborn errors of metabolism, but police baffled.

12 FEBRUARY

Met (Dr) Toby Hatchett in the golf club tonight, who asked me over a gin and ton if I'd seen 'The Doctor's Dilemma' on the box the previous evening.

'Oh, yes,' I told him. 'With Sir Bloomfield Bonnington stimulating the phagocyres like the Charge of the Light Brigade. The play couldn't possibly be written now, of course.'

'You mean, we no longer invent nuciform sacs for the rip-off of ripping them out?'

'Good heavens, no. Though luckily our nuciform sacs today are all psychiatric, which is less painful for the patients. But they'd have cured Dubedat, that artist fellow, in Act One. George! Another couple of gin and tonics, please, large ones. Nor today, Toby, would Mimi's tiny hand freeze in *La Bohème*. Or could Thomas Mann win the Nobel Prize with an enormous novel about life in a san up a Swiss mountain. Antibiotics may have conquered TB, but they ruined a lot of drama.'

(Had just exchanged *Wit and its Relation to the Unconscious* for *The Magic Mountain*, Miss Fludde concerned her bosom is growing larger, reassured her bra possibly shrinking.)

'I rather took umbrage at Shaw calling all professions conspiracies against the laity,' Toby complained.

'Oh, GBS imagined everyone else's job to be as easy as he found his own. Do you know, he never even *consulted* a doctor in his life. It's utterly amazing how he survived to the age of 94.'

'Cheers, Richard! But that mystique, that mumbo-jumbo, is as antiquated in medicine as the gold-headed cane. The patients know their rights like any other bunch of consumers.'

'I'll say. Last month I was threatened with litigation by the man who came to mend our washing machine, this month by the Ho Ho Ho! Oriental Takeaway.'

'Did you read about Sir Rollo in the papers? Stung hundreds of thousands of pounds for slicing off a pinkie in a moment's abberation. It's odd, but every patient who mistakenly loses a finger seems a potential virtuoso violinist, or a toe a future gold medallist Olympic sprinter.'

'Oh, yes, get your varicose veins done instead of your hiatus hernia, you're set for a world cruise. Your stomach removed instead of your kidney, retire to the Algarve. Have one of your elderly relatives knocked off, found a family business. It's the public's only source of untaxed cash in large sums, apart from the pools. I never understand why the judges swallow it.'

'Sheer spite,' Toby decided. 'The law is a profession as jealous as ours, but they all fall into our hands and we seldom into theirs.'

'And coroners –'

We both groaned. Doctors always groan at the mention of coroners, as schoolboys of the cane.

'They're impossible, of course,' I pointed out. 'Before taking the job they have to qualify in both medicine and the law, and fail in practising both.'

'Still, surgeons enjoy *some* privileges. Under the Royal College charter, I believe, their horses cannot be commandeered by the London fire brigade.'

'And being always on the move, they are similarly permitted to pee against the offside wheel of their carriages.'

'I don't know about the horses, but Rollo as a houseman tried the other one and got arrested. Mind, it was a No. 22 bus.'

I nodded across the oak-panelled bar, which has silver cups in glass cases and framed prints of the six golfing jokes. Old Townsend had come in. How tottery he looks, I thought. That's the cruelty of a club. Watching fellow members becoming infirm, with a sympathy made sincere through the awkward realization that we ourselves are growing as steadily grey, lined, bent and liable to fall downstairs or into the hands of the medical profession. Sandra describes the golf club as Churchford's most comfortable geriatric day centre.

'In the old days, if you recollect,' I resumed to Toby, 'surgeons could laugh off those mistakes they didn't bury. Remember what they taught us at St Botolph's? Damn near slaughter 'em and they're grateful for life, but they'll never forgive a scar not up to *broderie anglaise*.'

'Lost swabs are not nearly so dangerous in practice as loose women.'

'Rotten about poor Nigel, wasn't it?' I recalled. 'A GMC job, the lot.'

'He should have yelled for his receptionist as soon as the female dropped them.'

'With some female patients, I yell for my receptionist as soon as they drop their voices.'

'I came across an old French saying about priests, quoted by Sydney Smith — you know he was a medical student in Edinburgh, before switching to become a licensed wit? To adapt it for our times, there are three sexes — men, women and doctors.'

'One fact of professional life always puzzles me, particularly in connection with Mrs Noakes, who prepares herself for the doctor with the assiduousness of a Revue bar stripper for her audience. As we're mostly middle-aged, fat, bald and exhausted by bedtime, I can't understand why we're an aphrodisiac.'

'Women realize we see all their girlfriends undressed and want to go one better. You know what a keenly competitive sex they are.'

Toby sighed, like a man who has scaled Everest suddenly discovering he has no head for heights. 'I often wonder why we sweated six years to become doctors at all. Another gin and ton? My turn.'

'But wouldn't life be dreadfully dull for you and me if we weren't? Thanks, I will. How went the golf?'

'Bloody. Last night I looked up the muscles creating a perfect swing. Trapezius, deltoid, biceps, extensor pollicis longus and so on. I concentrated on the appropriate nerves to fire them off in the most effective sequence. The cervical plexus on the green, the brachial plexus in the bunkers. I hit everything into the rough or the next fairway.'

'In golf, as in medicine,' I reminded him, 'the best way to get out of trouble is to avoid it. And I've just remembered another line from that play, Toby. "No man who is occupied in doing a very difficult thing, and doing it very well, ever loses his self-respect." '

'I suppose that applies equally to medicine and golf, too. Cheers.'

'Cheers!'

Old Townsend joined us, to start talking about his arthritic hip. That their troubles fascinate the professional as readily as themselves is a touching belief of patients and golfers.

19 FEBRUARY

Heard no more from the Ho Ho Ho! Oriental Takeaway, but remembered that the mills of the law make those of God look like a high-speed dental drill. Had a long-standing golf game with Tom Blews, thought he'd cry off in shame, but he said lightly on the first tee that the Ho Ho Ho! Oriental Takeaway were good paying clients, *I* didn't feel personally involved in the treatment of my patients, surely, jolly painful for me if I was.

I complained he might get me out of the mess, instead of booting me further in. Tom said, easy. Go along and spend a few quid, enthuse to your fellow customers, I know my Chinese, they'll respond handsomely, probably give you an extra portion of crispy noodles. He added, it's not often you get free advice from a solicitor, ha ha, though he beat me three and two and took a tenner off me so it wasn't.

Met the major in the bar afterwards. Asked if he'd had a good game.

'Lost eight holes, four balls and my temper,' he told me. 'And I've a bone to pick with you, Doc.'

The point of any club is a mutual toleration of personalities and peculiarities, but the major when cantankerous is as irritating as ringworm.

'Was lifting my onions yesterday when the doorbell rang,' he continued over his Famous Grouse. 'Attractive young woman on the mat, thought she was collecting for the lifeboats, gave her fifty p. She explained – pretty stuffily – she was something called a health visitor. I informed her that my health was not open to visitors.'

'Ah, that was Susan,' I told him warmly. 'A girl as sweetly persuasive as Snow White with her Dwarfs, as long-suffering as Cinderella with difficult relations. She needs to be. Her job's health education, everything from senility to sex problems.'

'I don't know about the senility, but I had my sex education one night at Cairo in '43. Don't remember much about it, as we were all pretty pickled, but I ended up riding the donkey. Cheers!'

'Cheers!'

'You know, Doc, I can't abide this modern notion of nobody being trusted to shift for himself. The world's like a bloody holiday camp. No warbling in the morning bath, only at organized sing-songs. No laughing, except at the resident comic. If someone goes out in the rain, everyone must get wet. You take my point? I fought for King and Country, now I suppose it would be for Community and Society.'

'Well, World War One recruiting wouldn't have been so hot with Kitchener's face and "Your Environment Needs you".'

'It all makes me dreadfully gloomy. George! Two more please. With a left-wing government, everybody gets a job to do nothing, and the country goes bust. With a right-wing one, nobody gets a job to do anything, and they riot in the streets. Being Britain, we seem to have landed both.'

'One of our social workers proved to me yesterday that the mortality rate rises at double the unemployment rate. So I suppose when the dole queue hits 28 million, the problem will have cured itself.'

'You doctors simply add to the misery,' the major accused me. 'Why can't I make up my own mind about firing myself through the windscreen of my car? Having to wear a seat-belt is like being forced by law to wear a chastity belt. Don't you uphold individual liberty? Why must we be nannied from the cradle to the grave?'

'Remember Belloc!' I quoted, '"Always keep a hold of Nurse/For fear of finding something worse." Unfortunately, people choose the liberties they want to uphold as oddly as the women they want to marry. As for your car smash,' I corrected him, 'it is, alas, no longer a matter between you and me and the gate-post. Your fellow-citizens must fork out handsomely to keep you lingering on a life-support system.'

'What about this fluoride in the water?' The major continually writes letters to *The Times* about it, which it is as hesitant to print as his others about lack of moral fibre, arming the police, worsening of the climate through the disappearance of butterflies, etc. 'It might make me grow two heads.'

'Well, neither of them will get toothache,' I consoled him. 'A century ago, people were objecting as noisily as you to chlorine in the water, as an intrusion into the personal liberty to catch cholera. Why don't you join the Anti-Fluoridization Society? They've probably got a bar.'

'Mind you, I stopped smoking after the nasty scare.'

'That's one blessing you owe the medical profession.'

'It was nothing to do with medical profession. It was the fire brigade. I set myself alight in the loo.'

The major stared thoughtfully at his empty glass. 'I seem to be drinking twice as much of the hard stuff as ten years ago.'

'In common with the whole country. Very public-spirited of it. The government could never buy the Trident missile without the tax. Though I always advise that my patients restrict themselves to a couple of small tots per day.'

He looked shocked. '*You* don't.'

'If I did all the things I tell my patients, I'd be like a racehorse trainer living on oats.'

'The whole world's in a mess, Doc,' the major declared weightily. 'As for our individual liberty to do exactly what we like with our lives, even to end them – I think we'll feel it's better preserved if we stay put.'

'In this country?'

'No, in this bar.'

'Alcohol is a slow poison, but what's it matter? We're in no hurry. George! We shan't order any more. Just serve them up regularly. Cheers!'

24 FEBRUARY

Busy evening surgery, eight women think they're pregnant (six married) always a lot of it about at this time, due to dullness of TV programmes in New Year. Decided to take Tom Blew's advice. Directed Sandra smugly not to prepare dinner, we were having a special treat.

The Ho Ho Ho! Oriental Takeaway is identical to ten thousand others from Truro to Thurso. I neutralized staff's suspicion by slapping a wad of notes on the counter, made remarks suggesting the place a cross between the Savoy Grill and Champney's Health Farm, and ordered spare ribs, sweet and sour, pancake rolls, meat balls, cuttlefish, gizzards, bamboo shoots, hundred-year-old egg and so on.

Worked perfectly! Bowed out with everyone grinning, two carrier bags and complimentary chopsticks. If all medical contretemps were solved with such good-humoured open-mindedness, the Medical Defence Union would have to diversify into mail-order stethoscopes.

Annoyed, arriving home, to find my wife refused the feast, in fact declared shrilly she certainly wouldn't risk an attack of Chinese Restaurant Syndrome, and anyway it was only highly spiced garbage. It seemed that she had dressed up to dine at L'Epicurien behind the post office, further the washing machine had bust again.

Hurt, unappreciated, I countered that having paid for the stuff I was going to see it consumed. She said please yourself, I took the carrier bags into the kitchen, tipped them into half a dozen soup plates, Sandra sat across the formica and pointedly ate Weetabix. To my surprise, certainly to hers, I finished the lot, found it jolly tasty, particularly washed down with plenty of single malt and a bottle of Zagreb riesling, though abandoned chopsticks as like one-handed knitting.

25 FEBRUARY

Woke at 3 a.m. Agonizing colic. At least peritonitis. Probably dying. Considered ringing Sir Rollo Basingstoke in London, decided against it because remembered that surgeons generally cut the patient when called out of bed, and always when out of town, to justify the trouble and expense of journey.

My wife was utterly unsympathetic, as she blamed the riesling, told me not to make such a din retching, would wake Galen, probably the neighbours. Struggled to medicine cupboard, found what I hoped to be chalk and opium mixture, an excellent pharmacological cork. No label, but swigged half the bottle, not caring if I died during the remainder of the night from acute opium poisoning, or any other sort.

26 FEBRUARY

Windrush the pathologist at the General phoned this morning to ask if confinement of pregnant army officers should be to barracks. It seems I had thoughtlessly included in the maternity batch a specimen from the major.

When I related my symptoms (still as weak as a cholera victim), Windrush asked, hadn't I been to the Ho Ho Ho! Oriental Takeaway? Puzzled at this, not having mentioned my plan to anyone. When I told him yes, he split himself. Ho Ho Ho! Oriental Takeaway being closed at end of month by the council as a health hazard, kitchen full of dead rats, Windrush had seen them himself. I started about the Chinese Restaurant Syndrome, but he laughed heartlessly that I'd not got inborn error of metabolism but old-fashioned Tokyo Trots, Montezuma's Revenge, Delhi Belly, Rangoon Runs, Gippy Tummy or Aztec Twostep. In fact I was bloody lucky not to catch bubonic plague, typhus and rat-bite fever into the bargain.

Cut short the conversation. How pathetic, Windrush has not outgrown his medical student sense of humour. Determined to eat only in health bars, but had no defence against Sandra's insistence on dining out tomorrow at *L'Epicurien* (Paris prices).

Amazed at lunchtime to find Mr Tarwitch in the kitchen, surrounded by the washing machine. I asked coldly after his Guillain-Barré syndrome. He appeared lost. Persisted that he seemed dissatisfied with my diagnosis. He said amiably, oh all that, had to go to my own doctor, you see, Guv, because I wanted a sick note so's I could finish decorating my bedroom, kitchen and bathroom.

I despair of mankind. Were Socrates elected to the golf club, I should join him in a hemlock.

MARCH

1 MARCH

In bedroom this morning recalled remark of John Rowan Wilson (doctor–author). 'A man of middle life looking at his physique in the bathroom mirror. The flat feet, the varicose veins, the pot belly are there for good – he no longer has any hope of curing them. The most he can do is to cover them up.'

Depressing.

Such inevitable, irreversible inelegance – have I reached it? Do I make the Hunchback of Notre Dame look as cuddly as Orphan Annie? Am I sexually as incapable of arousing, and am I as unarousable, as a roast rooster? But Mrs Noakes (patient) acts passionately towards me at every opportunity. And I would act passionately towards Mrs Blessington (former local tennis champion), but never get the opportunity. A cheering thought came, which I passed to Sandra – the advantage of ageing is the daily increasing number of younger women. She replied it a simple effect of presbyopia – without my reading glasses I get an amazingly flattering view of wives at parties.

More depressing.

4 MARCH

To Manchester yesterday. Dinner at the Civic Club, commemorating twenty-five years of devotion to community by distinguished local GP, 'Groper' Gruby. Impressive speeches, Groper embodying highest ideals of noble profession, etc. Could not forget the pair of us thrown from Coat and Compasses opposite St Botolph's, through Groper's habit when plastered of crawling round on all fours looking up girls' skirts.

My London train cancelled this morning. Cursed. Next one grossly overcrowded. As left, man resembling boiled silverside, wife the dumplings, squeezed in beside me.

'Here we are, love, must be the last two seats on the train, would you mind shifting over a bit? We're off to London, annual excursion,' he started, seeming to assume we were lifelong friends. 'Not that it's much of a treat, the wife goes to Fortnum and Mason's and sees *The Mousetrap*, every time, enjoys it just as much, after all, you go and watch United play Saturday after Saturday, don't you? I just walk round looking at the flooring. Yes, the flooring. I'm in self-adhesive carpet tiles – in quite a big way, I'm not shy of admitting it, not shy at all – across at Chorlton cum Hardy. You're going to London I suppose? If you ask me, all Londoners are peculiar, rushing up and down the Underground like rabbits who've just heard that myxomatosis isn't a new sort of kitchen blender. Ah, see from your case you're a doctor?'

'I am in the profession, yes.'

'That's a funny coincidence. Last night, a young pal of mine developed a sore throat, had to speak in a whisper like this. See? So he went along to the doctor's, and the pretty young nurse answered the door, and my pal said, '*Is the doctor in?*' And she whispered back, '*No, he's out for a couple of hours, come inside.*' Eh? Eh? out for a couple of hours, come inside. Eh?'

'Oh, Doctor!' his wife revealed fondly, 'You ought to hear him at the Buffaloes, he's a scream.'

I clicked open my briefcase with the decisive air of switching off *Coronation Street*. 'If you'll forgive me, I must read this instructive *Times* leader. It's one of those filling the whole space beside the letters,' I indicated. 'Four-and-a-half feet of it, if you measure.'

I read, *In the hackneyed apology of Bagehot, the English are perhaps the least a nation of pure philosophers*...right down to *thus* quis custodiet custodes? *is today the phrase on every lip.*

'Doctor – this nurse, she was the cleverest nurse in the hospital. You know why?'

'No?'

'She could make the patient without disturbing the bed. She could make –'

'Thank you, but I *have* heard it, actually.'

'Edwin! Tell the doctor the naughty one you gave the Round Table. You know, about the girl who'd missed.'

'Oh, yes, you're going to enjoy this, being a doctor,' Edwin assured me. 'You see, a newly married couple went to their doctor, because the wife thought she was in the family way, and the doctor asked how many times she'd missed. So she looked at her hubby and said, "I don't think we've missed a night, have we, dear?" I don't think we've –'

'Would you kindly excuse me, while I read up some scientific research in this week's *Lancet*?'

I began, *A double-blind test of synthetic 1, 1-dichloro-2-(o-chorophenyl)-2-(p-chlorophenyl)-ethane was conducted in my wards....* Why do infuriating compulsive raconteurs imagine doctors mad on stories about doctors? How many mother-in-law jokes are actually *told* to mothers-in-law? The paper ended...*though the survey was most valuable, all the 1265 patients died.*

'Sorry, Doctor! Just meant that as a gentle nudge. Did you hear the one about the doctor who was sitting at home watching the telly late one winter's night? The phone rang and his wife answered it, see, and a patient said, "Can I speak to the doctor?" But he whispered across the fire, "Say I'm out on a case," so she said (he adopted the accent of an affronted meter maid) "I am most sorry caller, but my husband is out on a case." Then the chap on the line says, "This is urgent, can you go out and get him?" But the doctor's already shaking his head, and whispering, "Say you're in bed." So she says, "I'm in bed," and the patient says, "Is the man you're in bed with a doctor? Perhaps he may be able to help?" Perhaps he may be able to help! Perhaps he may –'

'I don't get it.'

He stared as though I had slighted Manchester. 'You don't?'

'I mean, I thought it was the nurse who whispered that the doctor was out for a couple of hours, and come inside?'

'Oh, no, no, no! You got it wrong. That was a different story. I hope you don't muddle up your prescriptions, Doctor? Eh? I hope you don't –'

'Edwin! Tell the doctor the one that made my brother choke.'

'Ah, yes, love. You see, the doctor told the fellow on the couch, "I can't diagnose your trouble today. Offhand, I'd say it was due to drinking." And the patient said, "Perhaps I'd better come back when you've sobered up." '

'Perhaps I'd better come back when you've sobered up,' I agreed. 'Quite right, too. Might I ask you to permit my reading this funny article in *Punch*? Thank you.'

Alone on a desert island, without even the Bible, Shakespeare and Roy Plomley... Cheshire sped past. There was a cartoon of a stockbroker standing on a window ledge. I read steadily to the pay-off...*my wife said, clearing up the splintered cocktail-sticks and pulverized cheese-and-onion flavour, 'It's the first time I've seen someone with curate's egg on his face.'*

'I've just remembered! A story that'll make you split yourself, Doctor –'

'Have you heard the one about the doctor who had one of his glamorous blonde patients say one afternoon, "Kiss me, Doctor"? "Kiss you!" he said. "If I kissed you, I'd get into the most awful trouble. I'd be up before the General Medical Council. Struck off. Lose my livelihood. Shunned by my friends. Disgraced by the public. Despised by my patients. Deplored by my colleagues. Disowned by my family. As a matter of fact," the doctor said to her, "I shouldn't really be in bed with you at all." I shouldn't be in bed with you at all.'

'Yes, yes, this one, Doctor, is about –'

'And the other one about the doctor who said to a stout female party on his couch, "Just move your buttock up." And she said, "My buttercup, Doctor? I've never heard it called *that* before." You see, she thought he was referring to her –'

'This is about a pretty girl who says to a doctor at a party –'

'I must read a significant editorial in the *Economist*.'

We repeatedly set the world to rights. If the world takes no notice...

'She says to a doctor at a party, "Are you a specialist?" and he says, "I'm a naval surgeon," and she says –'

'Edwin! You are a caution!'

'She says – but you're not getting off here, Doctor? It's only Crewe.'

'Just remembered. I've got an aunt in Crewe who needs to see a doctor. Good morning.'

'I always told you, love, London people are daft.'

Spent journey in corridor. Arrived home to find the major had disorganized the Hippocrates Answering Service.

8 MARCH

My birthday. Dozen golfballs from Sandra. Andy and Jilly from St Botolph's sent me a 'Get Well' card. Is this medical humour?

9 MARCH

Consulted this evening by Adrian, publisher. Has office in Bloomsbury, also writes books, lives in pink-washed cottage, wife pots. Cyril Connolly (obese man of letters) wrote of 'The chill wind which blows from English publishers, with their black suits and thin umbrellas, and their habit of beginning every sentence with "We are afraid…" ' But Adrian resembles agitated middle-aged elf, dresses with nonchalant carelessness which must take hours to achieve.

'Doctor, I'm dreadfully worried.'

'What about?'

'Everything.'

'Couldn't you start *somewhere*? Every consultation should have a beginning, a middle and an end.'

'Yes. It started when I stopped smoking, because I was worried about my lungs. Now I'm worried that the scare's a false alarm, and I've stopped the only thing which stops me worrying. I stopped drinking because I worried about my liver. That made me so worried I started again, and I worry that I drink more than ever. I go into pubs alone, worrying that I'm a latent homosexual. I look down my secretary's cleavage and worry I'm a latent rapist. Though I suppose those do rather cancel each other out, don't they? Worst of all, yesterday I found I'd mistakenly put on a pair of my wife's unisex knickers, and I'm terrified I'm a suppressed transvestite.'

'Don't *worry*, Adrian. The only harm transvestism ever did was to the menswear trade.'

'That's a relief, though I hardly thought eternal damnation could be bought for the price of a pair of Pretty Polly tights. But people *do* have such complex dirty minds these days, don't they? I'm absolutely tormented with worry about my insomnia.'

'Insomnia is only a pseudo-scientific term,' I reassured him, 'as meaningless as constipation or pornography. All depend on personal standards, generally cranky.'

'Are sleeping pills of value?'

'Enormously, towards the drug companies' profits. Why not retire with a good book?' I suggested wittily. 'I found a patient of mine reading your own *Luminous Grape* the other week.'

'How flattering.'

'Yes, it was such a pity he died when he was halfway through.'

'How I agree with you, Doctor. The best part was the ending.'

'My patients are even more obsessed with not getting enough sleep than with not getting enough sex. Did you know, wakefulness is caused by nerve impulses jangling in the brain like a flock of demented Buzbys? The natural state for man to pass his life in is sleep, so avoiding such items as World War Two and Rubik's cube. Were you a bat,' I pointed out, 'you could spend five-sixths of your life asleep, if you didn't mind hanging upside down. Were you a Malaysian tree shrew, you would never sleep at all, like Scotland Yard. Were you a cat, we could have you drop off by inserting an electrode into your head between your mammillothalamic and habenulopeduncular tracts; in labs it's happening all the time.'

'I've a terrific notion!' Adrian jumped up, snapping his fingers. 'Insomniac books! Sound asleep – no drugs – no side effects – recommended by the medical profession – endorsements from leading doctors. What works do you suggest? Gibbon? Boswell? Hume's *Treatise of Human Nature*? Proust and Rousseau? Any contemporary two-inch-thick American paperback? I see them now! Tastefully bound in midnight blue, we might give a free luminous bookmark.'

His mind is a pincushion of sharp, bright ideas.

I ventured, 'Did you know, Adrian, I used to run the St Botolph's student mag?' (Until an unfortunate misprint in the dean's pastoral poem – 'They lay in the long grass listening to the low, monotonous hum of incest in the woods.') 'I'm sure I could write a novel, if only, of course, I had the time. Can you give me any advice?'

'Don't. Writing novels, as Oscar Wilde said of landowning, gives one position and prevents one from keeping it up.'

I was perplexed. 'But the chat shows are always chatting up authors who make so much money they have to live somewhere where there's no cricket and the beer's all iced.'

'Only the clever ones. The author should look on the world not as his literate oyster, but as a vast comprehensive school. Write for the third form, make your fortune. It's far more difficult than writing for the sixth, which just isn't profitable anyway, even for those sensitive tales of tormented, neurotic Hampstead housewives.'

' "I do not know a better training for a writer than to spend some years in the medical profession," ' I quoted. 'And Dr Somerset Maugham surely ought to know? He stayed on the *Medical Register* to the end of his days, and could perfectly legally have delivered a baby, had the occasion arisen at Cap Ferrat and he'd happened to feel like it.'

'There must be something in the smell of hospitals,' Adrian admitted.

'I'm sure that of more use to Maugham than a first in Eng. Lit.' I agreed, 'was his Professor of Gynaecology's earthy remark – "Woman is an animal that micturates once a day, defecates once a week, menstruates once a month, parturates once a year and copulates whenever she has the opportunity." He thought it a prettily balanced sentence, too. How's the gout?'

'Not a twinge. I haven't touched a drop of port.'

'I keep telling you, gout is nothing to do with port. It's to do with purines. You eat them in things like sweetbreads and anchovies.'

'What about William Cowper's remark, "Pangs arthritic that infest/The toe of libertine excess"?'

'Forget it. Gout can occur in a teetotal athletic monk on a diet. Now, your anxieties. Why not see a psychiatrist?'

'Never!'

'Don't be coy. If you break a leg, you consult an orthopaedic surgeon. Same principle. Nothing shameful about having the appropriate specialist cure you.'

'That's what worries me,' Adrian protested. 'Suppose he did? If I'd nothing to worry about, I'd be worried right out of my mind.'

I prescribed a tranquillizer. A consultation with Adrian is a peepshow into another mysterious, sophisticated world of royalties, literary lunches and the Booker Prize.

11 MARCH

Mr McGregor storms from morning surgery after my refusal to prescribe whisky on the National Health. He asserts passionately Scotch only stuff to make him sleep. Somehow he has got hands on official *British National Formulary*, waves in my face Appendix 3, *Alcoholic Beverages* (*wines, tonic wines and similar preparations*). His trembling finger indicates, 'Where the therapeutic qualities of alcohol are required rectified spirit (suitably flavoured and diluted) should be prescribed.' What better description of Glenlivet, he demands emotionally, than that? Am adamant. Advised best remedy sharp walk with dog before retiring.

Why do some people regard the NHS as a statutory cure-all for their every ill from the nappy to the shroud, if mostly imaginary? Perhaps they have all read the lunatic definition of 'health' emanating from the World Health Organization in Geneva – 'A state of complete physical, mental and social well-being and not merely the absence of disease or infirmity.' When Thomas Mann's young hero said in the sharper air of Davos that he was, thank God, perfectly healthy, the doctor congratulated him, 'Then you are a phenomenon worthy of study. I, for one, have never in my life come across a perfectly healthy human being.' Me too. (Still reading *Magic Mountain*.)

Adrian sent this morning a purple-covered American paperback the size of a couple of pounds of Cheddar, *I Demand Satisfaction* by Ambrosine Dildo (I suspect a pseudonym). He seems serious about insomniac books, I hope not about the NHS supplying them, like Mr McGregor's Scotch, free on prescription. Adrian's note said, 'I think this a valuable addition to the cliterature.' Quite witty.

12 MARCH

This afternoon Mr Jorkin (builder and decorator) paid a domiciliary visit (as we doctors say) to inspect damp-course. Sandra says definite smell of dry-rot in kitchen, personally I think it dead mice under floorboards from her insanitary habit of leaving Galen's bikkies about. But agree to second opinion, any householder realizing that touch of dry-rot in skirting-boards means whole wall demolished, roof off, foundations dug up, scaffolding, probably bulldozers, vast expense.

Mr Jorkin, late thirties, leather overcoat, stylish beard, being a patient grabbed chance to cadge consultation without queuing. Limped through front door saying, 'I'm worried about my operation, Doctor.'

'My dear fellow, it's no more alarming than getting your hair cut,' I reassured him. 'Operating theatres these days are fearfully efficient. Crammed with electronics, printouts, liquid displays, television screens. The Honda production line has got nothing on them. You can hardly see the surgeons for the glittering machinery.'

'It's not the actual surgery, Doctor—'

'Ah, you're afraid something might go wrong? Well, I suppose it does from time to time,' I admitted. 'But don't fret, you'll stay in excellent hands. There's none of this hit-and-miss switching off the life-support system any longer. The famous *Panorama* programme put a stop to that. All those little tests to discover if you're really dead are now repeated after twenty-four hours, just to see if anybody's made a weeny slip. So if you sit up and demand breakfast in between, nobody should be in the slightest put out.'

'Naturally that's reassuring, Doctor, as I carry a kidney card.'

'Admirably public-spirited, but why stop at your kidneys?' I suggested, trying to head him towards the dry-rot. 'We can all be generous with the stuff we don't need any more. Just look at the junk that's unloaded on Oxfam. Cornea, liver, pituitary, heart…they all come in handy to the medical profession. Particularly as they're starting to use *two* hearts now per transplant. You probably saw it in the paper? There's inflation for you. In ten years' time, I suppose they'll be using three of four, hardly room for them all beating away at once, the thorax will resemble a can of worms. I'm just being fanciful, don't let me put you off,' I added, noticing him turning pale.

'My worry about my operation isn't that at all, Doctor. You see, with the waiting list at the local General, I'll be dead from natural causes before I've had it.'

'H'm, well, yes, it *is* rather a longer wait for new hips in this part of the world than for new Metros. I believe things are easier in Dundee,' I recalled from the *BMJ*. 'Why not sell your house and business, move to Scotland and start again at the bottom of the Dundee waiting-list? In the end, it would probably be quicker.'

'See here, Doctor, I've been doing pretty well in the trade – '

'Oh, I know, I know.' His bill for our double-glazing exceeded Chris' (in advertising) one for double hernia.

'I was thinking of having it done privately. Have you any idea of the cost?'

'Oh, shop round Harley Street for an estimate,' I told him lightly, seizing his elbow and towing him towards the rot. 'You know the sort of thing– "To sterilizing skin, making nine-inch incision, securing all bleeding points, inserting high-density polyethylene acetabulum constructed to British Standards specification, cementing with acrylic paste, making good, washing down, removing all tools from site, £2364.28." There's no VAT added, even if you don't pay cash.'

'I realize I've got to fork out,' he remarked thoughtfully, 'if I'm to be more comfy than the NHS.'

'Cheap at the price, I assure you. Private hospitals are just catching on that illness should be no impediment to expense-account living. You should see the menu from the Wellington Hospital, beside Lord's in London. Sixteen pages of it. Lobster Bisque, Tournedos Rossini, Canapés Ivanhoe… That's just one diet. They've also got low sodium, low fat, light or soft, which is more than you can say for Claridge's. The Wellie has a very drinkable Dom Perignon *Brut*,' I imparted. 'Free view of the Test matches, too.'

'I wouldn't be such a mug to rate a hospital on the booze and grub, no more than an airline. Safety first, I say.'

'True. But the fringe benefits are nice. Choice of TV channel in English or Arabic, separate sandwich menu for visitors, instant availability of chaplains from all denominations. Some people are bored to death in a private room,' I reflected. 'They like the trolley traffic, the sociability of a public ward, with plenty of folk anxious to chat about their own operations and offer their views on the surgeons, the cost of living, pornography, Spurs' chances next season, race relations and so on.'

Sandra appeared, suggesting a cup of tea. 'Ta, lovely,' he said. Infuriating. My entire afternoon would now be devoured by dry-rot. Mr Jorkin remarked, removing leather wear, 'These private hospitals seem to be springing up all over these days. Like garden centres.'

'They're a faster growth industry than space invader machines, since Barbara Castle toadied to the hospital porters' union and threw all private cases out of National Health pay beds. I hear BUPA are creating her their next 'Doctor of the Year', as the greatest booster of private medicine since Mrs Lydia Pinkham invented her famous Medicinal Compound, efficacious in every case. But perhaps BUPA's only joking.'

'I suppose BUPA *does* take the waiting out of aching.'

'If you want to save money, why not have your operation at home? It's the latest idea, in all the medical papers, to stop people eating their heads off in NHS beds. We doctors have given it a trial run at Bishop's Stortford. A bit of an upheaval, I suppose, moving the kitchen table to the bedroom, sterilizing the carpets, boiling up the instruments in the pressure-cooker, finding a 200-watt bulb for the lights, seeing the cats don't intrude in the middle of the proceedings. But if you can have your baby at home, why can't you have your cholecystectomy?'

'I'd certainly submit to the knife more happily in familiar surroundings,' he agreed gloomily.

'Sir Frederick "Elephant Man" Treves wrote a short story about a surgeon operating at home,' I recollected. 'The patient died. Unfortunately, it was his own home, and his own wife. In another of his tales, the relatives waiting in the drawing-room beneath were startled by blood starting to drip through the ceiling, a great patch spreading like a bottle of red ink spilt on the blotter. Jolly gripping stuff, take the paperback into hospital with you. Let's see, who's your surgeon?'

'Mr Crumleigh.'

'Oh, dear! He's not been too well recently. I'm afraid he's going to die before the pair of you can get together. Well, better you survive the operation than him, eh? Now, how about casting your professional eye over my brickwork?'

It wasn't dry-rot (relief). Apparently gas. The North Sea was steadily emptying into our kitchen. It was a wonder we hadn't been blown to smithereens, I'd better get on to the Gas Board quick, said Mr Jorkins, and left hastily.

21 MARCH

First day of spring, raining, Galen moulting badly, will insist on sleeping on consulting couch (warmest room).

22 MARCH

Hairs on couch upset lady with fibroadenoma, could not explain Galen damn sight more sanitary than many patients using it. Gas Board called, said not gas, probably leaking drains, better get builder to expose foundations. The construction industry leaves you as humiliatingly powerless as does the medical profession.

23 MARCH

Adrian reappeared this morning.

'Congratulate me, Doctor. I've just become a senior citizen.'

Amazing. Checked his card. Potting wife much younger. He'd probably had a few before. 'My dear fellow,' I encouraged him, 'you resemble a mature Byron in jeans, espadrilles and a batik shirt.'

'As an ex-publisher of twenty-four hours' standing, I've decided to accept the title graciously bestowed upon me by the government. Though I fear only as a semantic toupee. The patrician ring is nice, suggesting worshipful wisdom and civic responsibility. But my fellows who were queuing this morning at nine o'clock with their bus passes seemed indistinguishable from any other load of old buffers and dirty old men, or the dotards, crones and hags who were good enough for Chaucer.'

I expressed the opinion, 'We live in the euphemistic society, which is more dangerous than the permissive one. Camouflage the nasty realities of life, they still hurt when you run into them. Far better do the opposite, let broad daylight into our psychological nooks and crannies to flush out the bats of shame and guilt. Funny how I turn literary when you consult me.'

'Oh, empty phrases are always blowing across the paving-stones of language like crisp packets.' He waved his hand dismissively. 'Though honestly, I'd rather live in an underdeveloped country than an uncivilized one, believe me, cash-flow problems are definitely preferable to being flat broke. It's odd – before I got involved in publishing, I always thought that cash flow was a girl who worked in Liverpool.'

I mused, 'I don't really think that a patient feels any better for being handicapped rather than a cripple. Nor maladjusted rather than a rascal. Nor enjoying group therapy, instead of being a lunatic in an asylum. 'Asylum!' A word so gentle in sound and in evocation. And it certainly makes not the slightest difference if you're a terminal case or on the skids.'

'You know, I've been looking forward to this morning for forty-five years,' Adrian disclosed. 'At last I've time for all the things I've longed to do, though for the moment I can't recall what they were. Loss of memory's a sign of senility, isn't it?'

'Well, yes, with depression, worrying, apathy, fussiness, garrulity and an inability to look after yourself.'

'Had them all for years, dear boy. Quite a relief to quit publishing, I don't mind telling you. Alas, it is no longer an occupation for gentlemen, as once widely advertised. Authors are all getting above themselves – *you* try lunching one with something non-vintage. And all the famous publishing houses are owned by chisel-nosed accountants, who are simultaneously running defunct bus companies and motorway cafés and such horrible things. You probably noticed that Mr Rupert Murdoch, not content with grabbing *The Times*, was poised to take over the ancient publishers of Collins, so respectable they're licensed to print the Bible. Just imagine the Aussie influence – tucker from Heaven, turning the water into Foster's, the Twelve Cobbers, the Last Tea and the Sermon on the Hill. Do you know how the original Unwin once defined an Englishman's idea of a book? "A thing one begs, borrows, sometimes steals, but never buys except under compulsion." No change since 1926. I've been reading in the medical columns of the newspapers that the trauma of retirement is hardly less psychologically devastating than being born.'

'Well, there's a lot of it about. The British public, broken down by age and sex – as they rightly put it – is one-fifth over the age of sixty. Add another fifth under the age of fourteen and you see that half of us are slaving to keep the rest in idleness. With longer living from better medicine, plus the dole and redundancy, a man's working life will soon be a brief, confused episode in his existence, like his adolescence.'

'As I don't want to spend the rest of my days curled up with a book, I hoped you'd tell me lots of official schemes and things for doddering citizens.'

'Indeed, the State has the welfare of its elderly close at heart, for they may lose their teeth and their eyesight but never their votes.'

I reached for the glass-fronted bookshelf. 'Here's a most useful Pelican, the *Consumer's Guide to the British Social Services*. It seems to be fifteen years old, but I don't suppose the tracks in the welfare wilderness have changed much since.' (Decide I *must* bring my reference books up to date, but the years so flash by in general practice, it seems only yesterday I opened my latest edition of the *Medical Annual* – for 1962.) 'You can see from the list of contents how the benevolent government chuckingly elbows its way into Marriage and Family Life, bestowing Financial Help and Legal Aid, and offering Services for Special Needs, which sounds a bit Soho. How *did* our great-grandparents struggle through life doing it all for themselves?'

I flicked over the pages. 'Here we are, Special Services for the Elderly. Why, you can enjoy Aids for the Infirm, including loan of gadgets, Boarding Out of Old People, which embraces finding kindly lodgings. Almshouses any interest to you? Keeping warm I'm sure you'll go along with, though you might find Meals on Wheels a touch austere after all those lunches with authors at the Savoy Grill. Chiropody Clinics? Clubs daily, weekly or less often –'

'Definitely less often. Is there a more chilling term in the language than 'Geriatric Day Centre'? Jean-Paul Sartre's *Huis Clos* could have been set in one, instead of an ante-room to Hell.'

'You've only turned elderly overnight to suit the convenience of some indolent civil servants,' I consoled him. 'If everyone reached official retirement age only when they started going ga-ga, the country would be as difficult to run in an orderly fashion as the Grand National. You can obviously adjust a *mot juste* or turn a *bon mot* into *a mieux* one as deftly as yesterday.'

'Spending my days with a lot more old people I find utterly horrifying.' Adrian shivered. 'Quite as awful as running into a lot of Brits when abroad. Doctor – I've been considering an offer of a job. It's one full of frustrations and irritations, with appalling hours, continual disappointments, difficult human relations, and comparatively poor pay. I know because it's the one I've just officially retired from. What do you advise?'

'Start tomorrow. Could you let me have a few free books?'

30 MARCH

Adrian wrote to say insomniac books slickest idea to benefit mankind since the tin-opener and the crematorium. The Americans would go mad on it, they did with all literary gimmicks, bought blank books of wit and wisdom of their more thick-witted presidents. Just the promotional job to take thoughts off retirement, infinite thanks for putting him in mind of it, for which he'd be happy to let me in on ground floor, say an investment of £10,000, could I let him have a cheque by return, considerable overheads, etc.

Wrote back to say that insomnia could not catch me napping.

APRIL

1 APRIL

Dreadful shock this morning. As usual, open *Times* during coffee-break in living-room after surgery. At page three, strange feeling had read all news before. Increasing uneasiness, surely read it before – Economic Outlook Worsens, Appeal Court Judgement Angers MPs, Mincer Murder Verdict Today, Peer Denies Spanking, The Queen in Abergavenny.

Realize with alarm am suffering from what we doctors call *déjà vu* phenomenon, bizarre illusion of having lived through identical experience, rare but infallible symptom of tumours in the temporal lobe of the brain, which is just over your ears. Instantly saw self wheeled into neurosurgical theatre, clever fellows cutting brain about like slicing braised sweetbreads, left an imbecile, human vegetable, tragedy for whole family, patients devastated. Looked up, wondering whether mention it to Sandra and Mrs Shakespear, blissfully sipping coffee across the hearth, threw *Times* aside in fright. To my amazement, women fell about, Mrs Shakespear had inserted page of yesterday's paper, it being All Fools' Day. I pride myself that I can take a joke, even some of the major's, but this was not in the remotest funny.

4 APRIL

Sunday. Andy arrived in Alfa Romeo this evening with Hilda, stubble-haired, tomato-cheeked, wearing under bomber jacket T-shirt with scarlet map of Australia and I AM A VIRGIN, underneath, THIS IS A VERY OLD T-SHIRT. Tits like Miss Fludde's at the library, one jeans buttock had patch

47

reading DON'T RUBBISH AUSTRALIA, the other, C'MON POMMIES, C'MON. Assumed compatriot of Mr Murdoch.

From Trombone Creek, somewhere in open space between Brisbane and Darwin, staff nurse at St Botolph's on exchange scheme. Says beaut to visit genuine quaint old Pommie house, she personally not go along with view that if Aussies behaved like Brits, they could give the country back to the Abos and kangaroos for Christmas. Her grandpa Edgar was corporal – in a big hat over here in 1942, he talks frequently of lovely sheilas, Women's Voluntary tea, Vera Lynn, etc. Hilda explains everyone in 'Strilia imagines England now country hardly fit to graze saltbush weaners, bosses continually coming the raw prawn with trade union larrikins, though, mind, her dad gets as mad as a mule with a squib up its arse when he comes the bludger with that bunch of ning nongs – ta darl, she says, Andy handing her a half-pint glass of gin and ton.

I mention many famous doctors came from Australia. Like Florey. Can't remember any others. Andy asks to stay for tucker.

Chicken. Hilda says, 'Boiled chook, bloody good.' Asks, have I tried witchetty grubs? When fried, tastier than grasshoppers, though admittedly make sensitive people chunder. She once ate cockatoo, you boil it in a billycan with an axe-head, when the axe is tender the bird's ready to serve. Laughs like breaking surf. Sandra upset at half bottle of tomato sauce emptied over her cooking. Hilda confesses longing for dinkum Aussie hot meat pie, juice squirts in all directions when you bite it, like the way they used to castrate the lambs, her grandpa could ruin the sex life of half a flock in a morning, did I know his tobacco pouch was made from a kangaroo's scrotum? You just took the balls out and tanned it, he was more proud of it than Bradman's autograph.

Andy clearly fascinated with her, like as a boy with Evonne Goolagong. Before they left, took the chance of reminding him about the perils of marriage to persons of other cultures (if that not stretching a point). Andy asked, suppose I aware her dad multi-millionaire, biggest name in sheep since Bo-Peep? Said in that case she seemed a frank, healthy vigorous girl, hope he'd show her the Tower, Changing of the Guard, etc., bring her home whenever she felt like it, maybe we could find some witchetty grubs in Sainsbury's.

5 APRIL

Tricky case.

Mr Comfort appears at evening surgery, fat, pale, smooth-skinned, resembling vanilla blancmange in worn suit, stains down tie, one shoelace undone, glasses mended with Elastoplast.

'What I'm going to say will shock you, Doctor.'

'Impossible. We doctors are shockproof. Far more than any Roman Catholic fathers, and you don't have to blurt it out in such an uncomfortable and cramped posture. Paedophilia, pot, porn, poufs, Pakibashers – in our infinite Freudian compassion, we see such matter as interesting, often amusing, quirks of human behaviour.'

Slowly shook his greying head. 'Things are going badly, Doctor. The wife's run off with a younger man. Both the kids are in Borstal. Business is poor – I make decimal currency converters, and there doesn't seem much call for them these days. The TV tube's gone. I'm a lifelong Chelsea supporter. I'm so utterly wretched, I'm thinking of ending it all.'

Danger. Only way, try talking them out of it. But subtly.

'Jolly good idea.'

He seemed puzzled. 'You're not offended? Honestly? Snuffing the sacred flame of life?'

'Oh, there's a lot of euthanasia about this time of year. It's all the fashion. So you're going to kill yourself. How?'

'I've thought of all sorts of ways, but none of them strikes my fancy.'

'Ay, there's the rub. Have you read any Dorothy Parker?

Guns aren't lawful;
Nooses give;
Gas smells awful;
You might as well live.

Why not shuffle this mortal coil off Beachy Head?' I suggested helpfully. 'It's instant, once you make splashdown.'

'Fact is, Doctor, I took a single ticket to Eastbourne. But I had to come home, I've such a terrible head for heights. Could you offer something less dangerous?'

'My dear chap! For generations the medical profession has been making suicide painless, if not unnoticeable. You can do it by eating.'

'Eating what?'

'Just eating. Sixty years ago, clever actuaries working for life insurance companies calculated that anyone who weighed much over ten stone had a progressively curtailed life ahead. The fatter the shorter, get me? So if you eat four square meals a day, with hamburgers, bars of dairy milk, prawn-cocktail flavoured crisps and digestive biscuits in between, you'll be dead in no time.'

He looked despairing. 'Trouble is, Doctor, I'm so miserable I've lost my appetite.'

'Luckily, modern medicine means precise treatment. I agree, digging your grave with your teeth can be quite as hard work as lifting potatoes, but there's no longer any need to gorge indiscriminately. Stick to cholesterol,' I advised him. 'It's quite deadly. Makes Dyno-Rod jobs of your arteries in no time.'

'Do I need a prescription?'

'It's everywhere, all the really lovely dishes are *swimming* in it. Bacon and eggs. Fish and chips. Bread and butter. Steak and kidney. Strawberries and cream. Roly-poly and custard. Cheese and pickles. Cockles and mussels. Why, you're making me feel quite suicidal.'

'Living alone, I go in for tins, mostly,' he said gloomily. 'Baked beans, sardines, lychees and that.'

'Simpler still, then, stop eating fibre.'

'That a way of saying, stop chewing the rag?'

'Fibre comes in bran, brown bread, brown rice. It's just been discovered to be absolutely terrific for the liver and prolonging life in general. The medical journals are full of it. Though you'd better hurry up if you want to kill yourself by avoiding it, before we doctors discover that we're completely wrong, and every packet of muesli carries a Government Health Warning.' It occurred to me, 'You smoke, I suppose?'

'Never fancied it, Doctor. Not since I got the cane at school for Woodbines in the loo.'

'Take it up,' I recommended. 'Fags, naturally. Havanas are utterly useless – they're probably really just as dangerous as cigarettes, but not enough smokers can afford them to provide anything like reliable statistics. You drive?'

He nodded.

'*Never* wear a seat-belt. Do you realize, Mr Comfort, that such a simple, almost unthinking act as omitting to fasten your seat-belt every time you enter your car gives you a thousand extra chances of death a year! It's odd how MPs, and even ordinary balanced people, react so angrily against simple measures to keep them alive. You're not the only one with this problem,' I told him reassuringly. 'Freud was right, the whole world's drunk on thanatos. That isn't a tonic wine, but the death wish.'

'But I've got one of those cars which lets off a rude noise if your belt's unclipped.'

'Very well,' I continued decisively, 'we must find something else. As Webster said, "Death hath ten thousand several doors for men to make their exits." We don't need any of those societies of self-important busybodies to show us them, do we? Why not change your occupation? Men used to die from mule-spinners' cancer in Lancashire,' I ruminated, 'and hatters' shakes in Luton. Not to mention painters' colic in the Potteries, but I expect modern technology's blocked those loopholes. I believe mining and trawling are still dreadfully dangerous.'

'I suffer from claustrophobia and seasickness.'

'I expect there are other occupations just as risky but more comfortable,' I speculated cheerfully. 'The Atomic Energy Authority might be able to offer you something. Had a holiday recently?'

Mr Comfort's face lightened. 'I thought I might allow myself a nice break somewhere sunny, before doing it.'

'Excellent notion! Go to Spain. Catch Legionnaires' disease. Often fatal. Do you like Scotland?'

He nodded vigorously.

'Then take a fortnight on Gruinard Island, just off Wester Ross. It was salted experimentally with anthrax by the germ warfare boys in 1940, and they can't get rid of the spores. Though perhaps a fortnight would be a bit long,' I reflected. 'The incubation period's seven days, and it can kill you to the accompaniment of the most dreadful agony in the following three.'

'As you say, Doctor.' He sighed deeply. 'Though I must confess, I'm really an old stay-at-home.'

'There's no place like it,' I congratulated him warmly. 'Do you realize, more accidents occur at home than anywhere else? Just sit around, waiting for one to happen.'

Mr Comfort slowly rubbed a flabby cheek. 'There's one thing I find worrying about suicide. Supposing it doesn't work? Supposing I wake up in a nice clean bed in hospital?'

'Nowhere is more reliable for ending your life as swiftly as possible,' I encouraged him. 'Why, they needn't even give you the wrong drugs. Modern medicines, of course, cure most diseases, but with so many side-effects they generally kill you first. Hospitals are understandably crawling with antibiotic-resistant germs, because people bring them there especially. The doctors do so fiddle among your internal organs with needles, and tickle the inside of your heart with yards upon yards of plastic tubing, modern hospitals are quite as deadly as Scutari before the arrival of Florence Nightingale. It's called iatrogenic disease, because you catch it from a doctor.'

'Dear me, dear me! Death's more complicated than I imagined.'

'No, it's the simplest thing in life,' I corrected him. 'You can commit suicide by doing nothing more lethal than breathing. Travel in smokers – puffing a cigarette second-hand can be almost as nasty as one you've paid for. And lead! You're breathing it this minute, spewing forth as it does from every exhaust-pipe in the country, just to profit the oil companies. You know why the present generation of children is thick-witted and inclined to graffiti, insubordination and vandalism? Lead poisoning. Everyone says so. Well, everyone who hasn't any oil shares. Surely you've some asbestos about the house? A few deep breaths in its direction every hour on the hour will certainly do the trick.'

He wiped his brow with a dirty handkerchief. 'Doctor, this is making me more miserable than ever.'

Rising from my swivel-chair, I told him, 'Suicide can be *fun*! Have sex. Get the syph. In ten years' time you'll die believing you're the King of Siam.'

'Don't think I can wait ten years to die from anything. The missus might come back.'

I frowned. 'If you're in earnest, disappear with a pack of sleeping pills and a bottle of whisky, somewhere where they can't find you for twenty-four hours. Otherwise, they'll put you in an ambulance, then resuscitate you, which is dreadfully uncomfortable.'

'But I don't drink, Doctor!'

'Neither did the first patient I gave that advice to. He swallowed the whisky first, and the world looked so much better he decided to remain in it. He's now on three bottles of Scotch a day, pushing eighty-four. Otherwise, I can only suggest you go and live in Belfast or Beirut.'

He lifted himself from the patients' chair, 'Any other advice, Doctor?'

'Yes. The words of Winston Churchill – "It is never necessary to commit suicide, especially when you may live to regret it".'

'Maybe you're right, Doctor. Matter of fact, there's a new young lady typist come to work for me. Perhaps I'll ask her out to a movie instead.'

'I should. Good morning.'

'Good morning.'

9 APRIL

Good Friday. No more relieving human suffering till Tuesday. Hooray!

13 APRIL

8.30 a.m. back to work. Console self medicine the most intellectually exciting of professions, you never know what fascinating patient will next open the surgery door.

'Hello, Doctor! I'm bright and early, your first case after breakfast. I'd like a full and frank discussion about my sex life. I beg pardon, Doctor?'

'I was groaning about something else.'

'Had a nice weekend, I hope, Doctor?'

'Yes. Right-ho. Fire away. What's the hang-up?'

'I am, as you might say, twenty-three, a virile male, I drive a Ford Capri, second-hand, I have a steady employment in the retail trade. Yet I do not pull the birds. I have no charm. I do not pop corks.'

'Rotten luck.'

'Personally, I think it's my dad's ears.'

I had a flicker of interest. 'You mean, he bugs your telephone conversations with girls?'

'No, no! I've got 'em. Can't you see? Great flapping lugs, sticking out like radar dishes.'

'I must say, they're not particularly noticeable from here. But such things always seem far larger to the owner, like holes in the teeth or trousers.'

'I have been contemplating plastic surgery.'

'Have you?' I asked shortly. Mr Parfitt was thin, with a pale complexion, pale blue eyes, and pale sandy hair, as though he had faded steadily over the years, like our chintz living-room covers. For centuries, sex has soaringly inspired European literature and art, but in my practice seems to cause more trouble than indigestion. 'There's such a waiting-list, by the time you get your ears pinned back on the NHS you'll have hit the male menopause.'

'I had a little win on the pools I've been keeping quiet about at work,' he confessed slyly. 'I'd thought of using the private sector, as people say.'

'Nothing easier. There's a dreadful fuss in the profession at the moment about "cowboy clinics", which seem to be springing up all over, like McDonald's. I wonder why raffish entrepreneurs should always be cowboys?'

My gaze wandered to the bird settled on the window ledge. Was it a chaffinch? 'I imagine cowboys as placid, milk-fed Thomas Hardy characters, sucking a straw, don't you?'

'Could you tell me a nice one?'

'Nice what? Oh, clinic. No need. Go out and buy *Vogue* or *Queen*. They advertise. That's what gets up the profession's nasal sinuses. No ordinary surgeon would ever dream of advertising. Not in the glossies, anyway. Mind, you won't find your clinic much like the Princess Grace Hospital in the West End. More likely a Hampstead flat, maybe a semi-det in Ruislip. In America, they do it in suites in hotels – you know, Rib Room one way, Cosmetic Surgery the other.'

'But do you suppose they'd take on my ears?' He fondled them, as a mother her loved but wayward twins.

'If you pay enough money – they like it first, by the way, and I expect in cash – they'll not only trim your ears but carve them with decorative scrollwork. While you're there, if you feel like it you can have a nose bob, a wattle job on your neck, eyes debagged, crop of hairplugs planted across blighted patches, maybe a brow lift.'

'What's that?'

'They jerk your forehead towards the nape of your neck and keep it in place with metal staples. If you were obese, you could have your weight sliced away like the canteen butter, much less tedious than dieting. If you were female, they'd make you a smashing pair of silicone Charleys, any size you like, pomegranate to pumpkin.'

'Does this sort of surgery hurt, Doctor?'

'Frightfully! But thousands of people face it with a stiff upper lip, if that's the right phrase. In California, it's so popular that almost the entire population look different from the way they really are. I don't know if it makes them any happier, or their spouses any sexier. There's a North Country expression, "If you're doing badly, paint the cart." But the same old nag's got to haul it along.'

After a silence he asked hopefully, 'Do you suppose my trouble's all in the mind?'

'H'm. How about your dreams?'

'Well I'm always having this one about flying somewhere from Luton.'

'There you are!' I told him triumphantly. 'Freud pointed out that balloons and Zeppelins – he was lecturing before the jet age – are male sex symbols. The amazing defiance of gravity comes into it, but we needn't elaborate at this hour of the morning. Sex and flying is a terribly common modern fantasy. *Emmanuelle* did for aircraft loos what sliced bread did for the bakery trade.'

'My last girl left me because she kept dreaming I was chasing her through the rain with my umbrella.'

'Freud would certainly suck his teeth about that,' I told him severely. 'Umbrellas, knives, spears, rifles, watering cans, fountains, church spires – even fishes and snails, for some reason. And on the receiving end, as it were, cupboards, velvet-lined jewel-boxes, stoves, whole rooms. Sexual symbols, the lot. It's in the same lecture, with the Zeppelins.'

'If you ask me, Doctor, everything can be related to sex. After all, most of us are thinking about it most of the time.'

'That's why Freud couldn't lose,' I agreed. 'How's your relationship with your parents?'

'Don't see much of them since they got the geriatrics and went to live in a mobile home parked at Reculver.'

'Maybe you're suffering from an Oedipus complex? You want to castrate your father and marry your mother.'

'Coo, Doctor.'

'Don't worry, everyone has it. Infants, quite nastily. Hamlet was a shocking case. It's Freud's idea, of course. He got it on 15 October, 1897. Personally, I find it a jolly comforting notion. When parents complain to me their children are difficult, I just think what the little brats would do if they let rip their fundamental instincts. Though I expect in your case, you only want to cut off your father's ears.'

He continued shamefacedly, 'You know about sex shops, Doctor?'

'Since my days as a ship's surgeon,' I assured him. 'Yokohama and Kobe were full of them, long before the world learned to pronounce Sony and Datsun. My captain was less furious at catching a dose from his Japanese rubber mistress than at her violation by the mate while he was ashore.'

'I went to one actually, up in London. There was a machine like a pint milk bottle with a red rubber bulb, for enlarging the size of what you might call the organ.'

'Alas, anatomically impossible.'

He looked disappointed. 'Also, sort of accessories you fit to it, like nudge-bumpers to the car. In the end, I settled for a French tickler and a knitwear willie-warmer. Also some Casanova's Black Pearls, guaranteed to contain the vital constituents of twenty-five large oysters.'

'Cheaper than taking the girl out to dinner at a Mayfair oyster bar.'

'Mind, I wouldn't look on any woman as a sex object.'

'My dear Mr Parfitt, we are all digestive objects, or we would waste away. We are all respiratory objects, or we would suffocate. We are all sexual objects, whatever the more noisy females say. Otherwise there would be no more us.'

'Perhaps I'll just buy a body-developer and use it in the intimacy of my own bedroom.'

'Good idea. I'd suggest coming back in a year, but you'll be married by then. Statistics are more reliable than surgery. Good morning.'

15 APRIL

I had an overpowering feeling of impending doom all day. Something dreadful was going to happen to me. But nothing did. Strange.

24 APRIL

Still worried when think of Mr Parfitt. Could have been more helpful, suggested he sprayed himself all over with androstenone aerosol, mysterious male sex pheromone, discovered by keen-eyed doctors noticing that female students took seats just vacated by males, one whiff on lapel said to attract women like solitary West Ham scarf on Arsenal terraces. Same method that Othello used to bewitch Desdemona, according to her father, and probably would lead someone like Mr Parfitt into much the same trouble.

Another sex case this morning, son of prosperous local dentist.

'Why it's young Clive. Good to see you. What's the trouble? Tennis elbow, athlete's foot or saddle sores? I'm always reading in the local paper how you go great guns at the gymkhana.'

Concern marred a face as pink and as fresh as a newly opened yoghurt. 'I'm to be married, Doctor.'

'Congratulations! Who's the lucky lass?'

'The girl next door. Mummy and Daddy are awfully pleased. Hers, too, of course.'

'Getting married is surely an occasion for consulting your conscience rather than your physician?'

'Fact is, I'm worried. Frightened. Terrified.'

'Really? But I always thought you as enviably self-confident as a disc jockey.'

'Oh, I know I'm called locally "Cocky Clive",' he agreed modestly, 'but…well, Doctor, it's different from my usual larking about isn't it? I mean, being alone with a woman you don't know frightfully well for a whole night.'

'As the old English proverb says, more belongs to marriage than four bare legs in the back of a Ford Fiesta.'

'The ceremony's being performed next Saturday.' He seemed to be contemplating major surgery. 'How do I behave in our bedroom of the Groyne View Hotel, Southsea?' he asked desperately. 'Come to that, how do I behave in the sun lounge of the Groyne View Hotel, Southsea? I've never in my life stayed at a dump like that, full pension including English breakfast and afternoon tea.'

'Couldn't you switch to somewhere more romantic? St Tropez, St Ives, St Neots?'

'Mummy and Daddy insisted, because they honeymooned there while Daddy was doing his national service in the Dental Corps.'

'Everyone panics at making a fool of themselves on their honeymoon. Cheer up! It's not quite so bad as Leonardo da Vinci said – "The act of procreation and everything connected with it is so disgusting, that mankind would soon die out if it were not an old established custom, and if there were not pretty faces and sensuous natures." Rather melancholy, even for a *quattrocento* queer.'

'I could do with a bit of practical advice, I must say.'

'I give the same to chaps making their first speech at the Rotarians. Stay sober and don't try being too clever, and you'll sit down to a round of applause.'

'Dora's absolutely delish, but she's in the leading-rein class sexually. That's why I'm marrying her,' he pointed out. 'I couldn't possibly marry any one of those birds I've been knocking about with, could I?'

'Luckily, the medical profession is as well furnished with advice upon this as on other human predicaments. I've a few books somewhere in the surgery –'

I reached for the bookshelf.

'Here we are! The very thing. *Getting Married*, guidance from the entire British Medical Association on how to do it.' I noticed with surprise the price, two shillings. 'The 1966 edition. H'm. Well, the principles can't have changed since the Garden of Eden. And according to one of the country's most popular novelists, our ever-romantic Miss Barbara Cartland, the old pre permissive virtues are returning, virginity and all that. Forty-two chapters,' I noticed approvingly, turning the pages. 'Packing for your honeymoon... Buying a House... Making your Bank Work for You... Shopping for Storage Units...for Cutlery...the BMA's a very practical organization, you understand.'

'Daddy warned me to take care, because wives have their honeymoons on instant recall, like your life flashing before your eyes when drowning.'

'Personally, I agree with Noël Coward that honeymooning is a very over-rated amusement. Like Christmas.'

'Mummy says her feelings on honeymoon from beginning to end were exactly the same as the day she met Daddy.'

'How charming.'

'He was filling her teeth.'

'The chapter on *Enjoying Each Other* might be what we're after,' I suggested. ' "This can make itself felt even in the smallest everyday occurrences, like a man saying, 'Ah! That's very good,' when his wife hands him a cup of tea." Perhaps we'd better try something more permissive.'

'Hope you don't mind me lumbering you with this, Doctor?' Clive apologized. 'But you've known me since I wore my first hard hat.'

'Not a bit, it's extremely refreshing, giving advice which doesn't simply tell the patient to stop whatever he likes doing. *The Joy of Sex*? At least it's in decimal currency. Lots of tasteful pictures, though I must say they don't seem to be enjoying themselves much more than the couple in the St John's Ambulance manual illustrating resuscitation of the drowning. Masters and Johnson? The Americans bring an admirably analytic seriousness to sexual gyrations as to those of Wall Street. *Sexual Behaviour in the Human Female?* Read all about it in 863 pages, from Abelard to the Zuni Indians. What *could* Zuni Indians do? Oh, transvestites, though I doubt if it was particularly noticeable.'

Clive looked doubtful. 'Could you suggest something a bit simpler? Dora's not much past *Blue Peter*.'

'This is it! Look – *Ideal Marriage* by Dr Van de Velde, first published in 1928, the same year as *Lady Chatterley's Lover*. Well furnished with line drawings, stark but useful, like the map of the London Underground. Aphorisms, too,' I noticed. '"Without marriage there is no happiness in love", Madame de Staël. Now you know.'

'I think I'll have to treat it like trying for a clear round at the gymkhana.'

'I should. Don't fall off. Good morning.'

29 APRIL

Appallingly busy day. Always is before Bank Holiday weekends. Patients apparently stocking homes with drugs as frantically as with food. All those going abroad cadging prescriptions against seasickness, squitters, syph and other diseases rife among foreigners with dirty habits. Complicated by Sandra complaining of splitting headache, examined her briefly in kitchen, told her merely neurotic, she burst into tears, and pointed out that President of BMA just declared suicide rate among hyperstressed doctors' wives was 458 per cent of that among rest of population, it was in *World Medicine*. Felt awful, but family of busy cobbler must go slipshod.

30 APRIL

Woke with terrible headache. Sandra not sympathetic, particularly as knows exactly what I'm suffering. My case of course *not* neurotic. Look up 'Headache' in textbook index, 23 causes, not including skull fractures and head lice. The terrible curse upon we doctors – while many ordinary folk still think heart seat of emotions, brain throne of reason, etc, we know them to be complex electro-chemical computers liable to sudden inexplicable breakdown. Decide probably got saccular aneurism of circle of Willis, Sandra will be sorry when I'm gone, Galen too.

Before surgery phone (Dr) Toby Hatchett for consultation, wife Paula says Toby suffering acute lethargy, has taken week fishing for salmon in County Cork (where presumably disability unnoticeable). Do not care to consult locum (wise man from the East), nor apparently does Paula, tells me she woke suffering dreadful backache, what do I suggest? Not much, woman being defined as a constipated biped with pain in the back. End month gloomily, though little time for self-diagnosis as overwhelmed with patients. The busy cobbler must stick to his last. To his last...

MAY

8 MAY

Drive across town to (Dr) Toby Hatchett, now back from County Cork. Surprised to find him in consulting room seemingly doing scientific work down small microscope, but is tying fishing flies.

'Come in, Richard. So you got away from your surgery? Good! Getting on for one o'clock. Curing the sick *en masse*?'

I smiled. 'To cure sometimes, to relieve often, to comfort always, that's our job. Well, according to Dr Trudeau of the Adirondacks.'

There was a silence, broken by Toby asking, 'How's the family?'

'Fine! Sandra's fine. Andy's fine. Jilly's fine.' Another silence. 'The dog's fine.'

'Lovely day, eh?'

'Magnificent! The cow parsley will soon be out.'

'Really?'

More silence.

'And how's *your* family?'

'Oh, fine.' Toby fiddled with his smart silvery ballpoint. I had one, too. It commemorated the pharmacological breakthrough of Super-tranquer. Or maybe Burpeeze Babyfood. 'Do sit down,' Toby invited suddenly.

His patients' chair. Spindle-backed Windsor. Striped plastic cushion. The embarrassing but inescapable moment. Hercule Poirot inviting his host the baronet to explain his movements the afternoon her ladyship was dismembered in the library.

'I'm enormously flattered to treat a fellow GP,' Toby volunteered, 'but dreadfully sorry you're in trouble. Nothing serious, I hope?'

I replied gravely, 'I'm afraid so. McArdle's syndrome.'

'Ah. Yes. McArdle's.'

'I'm sure you know far more about it than I do,' I confessed hastily.

'No, no, my dear chap! I'm sure *you* are a complete expert on McArdle's syndrome. Perhaps you'd...er...sort of refresh my memory?'

'Cramps due to low blood lactate from deficiency of muscle phosphorylase. I just looked it up. Terribly rare – as you're aware, naturally.'

Rule for conversation between doctors – where shared ignorance is bliss, 'tis folly to pretend you are any wiser.

'It started last week with headaches,' I gave the case-history. 'But the symptoms developed when I was playing golf yesterday, on the sixteenth.'

'That really is an infuriating hole. How did you do?'

'I took four. Not bad, eh? Playing Jim Humbles, the town clerk.'

Toby grinned. 'Who treated the round as an *al fresco* consultation?'

'I'll say. Started with his bowels on the first tee, the old ticker on the dog-leg second, and his insomnia and sexual fantasies saw us through the rest of the round. Incredible, the number of hypochondriacs at large, isn't it? They make more trouble for us in the profession than false alarms for the fire brigade.'

'Doesn't Jim wear one of those copper rings round his wrist against rheumatism? He's the sort of chap who'd no sooner sit on cold stones than on a wasps' nest.'

'The public's so pathetically muddled about its health.' I shook my head sorrowfully. 'It wasn't all that long ago since country folk round here were curing sore throats by rubbing the patient's head with a roast potato.'

'Might I ask you to drop your trousers?'

I unzipped. 'Going to the reunion cocktail party at St Botolph's next Friday week?'

'Of course,' he said enthusiastically. 'Odd, isn't it, how English doctors look on their old hospitals as their old schools? The Americans can't understand it.'

'Oh, to the Americans Billy Bunter's just another case of Froehlich's syndrome.'

'It's chilling to realize that all those larks – remember the awful business of snipping the theatre sister's knicker elastic when she was scrubbed up on a case? – were perpetrated when you and I were younger than our sons are now.'

'How old *are* you, Toby?'

'Same age as you,' he replied promptly.

'I always remember Maurice Chevalier. "Never resent growing old. Think of the many who are denied the privilege." '

'I can only remember Clem Attlee, when people asked how it felt to be eighty – "Wonderful, compared with the alternative." '

I stood with my trousers round my ankles, like the theatre sister's knickers. 'What shall I do?'

'Better get up on the couch, I suppose. Like an ordinary patient, however *infra dig.*'

'A much more expensive couch than mine. Very comfy,' I observed. I gave a deep sigh. 'Shaw was right. The most tragic thing in the world is a sick doctor.'

'Well, the most ridiculous.' Toby gazed at my lower half as Moses upon the face of the Lord. 'When we're ill it always amuses the patients, like the idea of the police station being burgled.'

'Yes, I think even the nicest patient feels a glow of satisfaction when his doctor drops dead. It's like winning at poker.'

'Your legs look pretty normal, to my completely inexpert eye. But Richard, as we do happen to be in the same consulting room, could I consult *you*? I'm suffering from hypokalaemic familial periodic paralysis.'

'Phew! You don't say? What is it?'

'Attacks of weakness of the skeletal muscles precipitated by a high carbohydrate intake, associated with low serum potassium and inherited in an autosomal dominant fashion. Very uncommon.'

'Funny, isn't it, how we doctors never get the ordinary diseases our patients do?'

'I thought I was just tired, so went fishing.'

'Catch anything?'

His eye glinted. 'Incredible! Forty-pound salmon. Got it on a Swedish prawn wobbler.' He spent five minutes demonstrating with a rolled-up *BMJ*.

'How about that Sri Lankan locum?' I enquired. 'Reliable?'

'Reasonable. Except for prescribing an expectorant cough mixture to some poor chap who complained he couldn't get it up. If you shift over,' Toby suggested, lowering his own trousers, 'I'll strip off and you can have a look at *me*.'

'Certainly, old man.' We changed positions. 'Though of course I know nothing about…whatever it was you said you had. To my totally unpractised glance, you look as healthy as Tracy Austin.'

'I'm not certain I haven't a touch of Swiss-type agammaglobulinaemia as well,' he added nervously. 'Just read a paper about it in that *BMJ*. Invariably fatal.'

'I'd prescribe total abstinence from the *BMJ*.'

'You don't really think I've got it?'

'If you had, I shouldn't be able to diagnose it, so what's the odds?'

'To decide you're suffering from a killing disease and finding you're not, is rather like being dropped by St Peter in the slips,' Toby reflected.

'I don't know what to advise you about the McArdle's syndrome.'

'Hang on, Richard – isn't it you who's got the McArdle's syndrome? I'm the hypokalaemic familial periodic paralysis.'

'These obscure complaints are terribly easy to muddle. I don't suppose it matters much. There's never any cure for them, because they're too obscure for anyone to bother finding one.'

'We'd better exchange *some* treatment.' We both pulled up our trousers. 'It would be like a couple of bishops meeting and not blessing each other.'

'Whenever I'm ill, I take a handful of the latest tablets the drug salesman happens to have left in the surgery,' I told him.

'Care for these? The chap assured me they're the greatest thing since sliced manna.'

'No, they're purple. I never swallow purple capsules. A clinical principle as sound as any, I'm sure you'll agree.

'Well, these tranquillizers, which apparently turn the world into instant Disneyland. Or perhaps you'd prefer not?'

'What about those striped ones, like bottled wasps?'

'Oh, no! They've got more side-effects than Boadicea's chariot.'

'Despite the drug reps' scientific jargon, their stock-in-trade's largely indistinguishable from H G Wells' Tono-Bungay, Aldous Huxley's Soma or P G Wodehouse's Buck-u-uppo, which turned bishops into rather rowdy fifteen-year-olds,' I suggested.

' "The desire to take medicine is perhaps the greatest feature that distinguishes man from animals" – our eminent Edwardian Sir William Osler may be right. How did our fathers cure their patients by giving them only rhubarb mixture?'

'Because they wrote the prescription in Latin. The food's always more impressive if the menu's in French.'

'It's a sound clinical principle of *mine*, Richard, to prefer drugs which are well established. Say, since the time of Noah's Ark.'

'It's lunchtime. And it's Saturday.'

'Gin and ton?'

'I'm sure it will do us both the world of good.'

12 MAY

Discovered, leafing through a Price's *Medicine*, that 'Pinta' is a disease. Contagious, attacks either sex, all ages. 'Patches of pigmentation are first noted on the back of the hands or face, from which they spread elsewhere: they are somewhat rough, dry and raised, and vary in colour, red, violet, white and black.' I do hope the Milk Marketing Board knows.

15 MAY

Wedding anniversary. Saturday, so Andy and Jilly could come for dinner (*L'Epicurien*). Ordered *carré d'agneau à la bordelaise*, Andy shuddered, said prefer fish and chips, even baked beans. Puzzled. He says, remember Hilda? Well, sheepmeat exhausts all possibilities as sole topic of conversation in well under a fortnight, added opaque remark that now he knows how a male kangaroo feels during rutting season, and why it needs a lot of room.

Jilly dissecting head and neck. Have slight argument over the *fraises des bois* about complicated course of the lingual nerve round salivary duct and small muscles under the tongue. I quoted firmly and loudly,

The lingual nerve
Took a swerve
Around the hyoglossus.
'Well, I'm fucked,'
Said Wharton's duct,
'The bugger's double-crossed us.'

Jilly flattened, realizes the old man not such a fool as thought. Most gratifying.

21 MAY

'Rollo! Good to see you. Congratulations on the gong.'

'Thank you, Richard. I'm sure a single-handed GP merits one more than a consultant surgeon like myself with a pack of keen young hospital registrars baying after his work.'

'Maybe I have one? I never check the Honours List. Do you claim by telegram, like the pools?'

'Well, the prizes are awarded on much the same system. You remember Dr Puskett, who gives my anaesthetics?'

'Old Pubis Puskett! You haven't changed a bit. You gasmen have become terribly important chaps, haven't you, since the rag-and-bottle days when you knocked 'em out and did the crossword. But I can never forget that line from *The Doctor's Dilemma* – "Chloroform has done a lot of mischief. It's enabled every fool to be a surgeon."'

'Ha, ha,' said Sir Rollo (didn't think him overmuch amused). Now justifies name 'Rolly-Poly' – thick, wavy grey hair indicating wisdom, even patronage of Trumper's, heavy black-rimmed glasses as chosen by TV interviewers and trade union leaders to indicate weighty sense of responsibility, Savile Row suit suggesting Rolls outside, country place, gentleman's club, Krugerrands. 6.30 p.m. in St Botolph's Governors' Hall (early eighteenth century, oak-panelled, scrolled pillars, coffered ceiling, portraits of dead doctors), crowded, noisy, typical doctors' party, nobody smoking and everybody getting as pissed as arseholes.

'It's fascinating at these reunions to see who's won the lollipops or the lemons,' I continued to Rollo. 'Always fun to rerun the old days, isn't it? But at our age, it's rather like dropping into the local during the Black Death.'

'Indeed, these affairs do rather rub home that a man is as old as his arteries. I must say, I'm not mad about entering Heaven to a reception committee of my unsuccessful patients.'

'You should have been a judge,' I suggested, 'his discontented clients by definition going to Hell. Who's the chap looking like the last archbishop but one?'

'Flewby. President of the Royal College of Therapeutics.'

'Filthy Fred Flewby? Impossible! The fellow he's talking to, who could be Mr Gladstone's elder brother, surely isn't Quack-Quack Duck?'

'President of the Royal College of Laparotomists.'

'I wonder if they're reminiscing about that rugger tour of the West Country? They shared a hotel room, and in the middle of the night Flewby woke with a hyperextended bladder – I personally saw him sink twenty-two pints of Devon ale – and finding nowhere else, decided with alcoholic devilishness to use the suitcase under Duck's bed. Went to sleep hugging himself with glee. In the morning, found they were so tight they'd got into the wrong beds and he'd got the wrong suitcase.'

'Richard! *Dear* Richard!'

Facing dowdy middle-aged woman never seen in life.

'If you've forgotten me, I'll be absolutely furious,' she declared.

'Forget you? Forget *you*?' Raked her for clues. Shapeless purple suit, frilly blouse, brooch like horse-brass. Hearty ward-sister when I skittish student? 'I could *never* forget you…er…Mrs Er…'

'Claypole.' Added oozily, 'But *you* knew me as Flopsy-Wopsy.'

Slapped brow. 'Of course! Who else? Flopsy-Wopsy.'

'On your night-rounds as a houseman, Richard, when I was an innocent young nurse, in the hospital barely six weeks –'

'May I introduce my wife?' Sandra had come out of the scrum at the bar.

F-W continued enthusiastically, 'You were absolutely *wicked* – '

'Er, my wife – '

'Wicked! Wheedling me to cook you bacon and eggs in the ward kitchen.'

Bacon and eggs! It all came back. '*Now* I remember, Mrs, er, Wopsy. You were a tiny blonde thing – '

'I *have* put on rather a few stone, but you needn't be cruel about it, you naughty boy.'

Luckily, she distracted by *vol-au-vents*. Squeeze Sandra among crowd like jellyfish through seaweed.

'Who was that?' she asked, puzzled.

'Night pro on gynae.'

'Really? I remember *her*. She used always to smell sweaty even then.'

Facing small square man with beard. 'Piggy Pendergast?' I enquired amiably. 'Absolutely the live wire of our year! Always up to the highest jinks. Didn't I hear you're a professor?'

'Mm. Yes. Doing some very interesting work on kwashiorkor. Tell you all about it. The name "kwashiorkor" comes from the language of the Ga tribe in Ghana. It means "first-second". You may well ask why. I'll tell you. The Ghanese mother, when breast-feeding the new baby, only then weans the elder one. For this purpose, she feeds it a gruel, made from a traditional tribal recipe. Now this I think the utterly fascinating part. The gruel is deficient in protein. Quite significantly so. You follow? I'll explain. The people of the Ga tribe of Ghana live on staples – plantains, cassava, maize – which are adequate in carbohydrate, *perfectly* adequate in carbohydrate, but protein-poor – '

'Thanks, Rollo!' I grabbed the glass. 'A gin and ton, superb, thank God for the life-belt. Isn't an expert someone who bores more and more about less and less?'

Rollo groaned. 'I object to being given a lecture on tropical sprue, simply because I happened to be peeing next to that fellow in the gents.'

'Surely the chap pouring himself a Perrier can't be Wizard Tizzard, who won the gold medal for medicine *and* surgery?'

'Yes. He exists at the end of an even more specialized isthmus than Piggy. The Calvinist Home for Recidivist Alcoholics on Exmoor.'

'He runs it?'

'He's in it.'

'Why, it's old Richard!' Small, bent man in green velvet suit, total stranger. 'You went off to be something ridiculous like a ship's doctor, didn't you?'

'Yes, I was a sort of floating doc for a bit,' I quipped.

'And now?'

'I'm in practice at Churchford. You know, stockbrokers pretending to be farmers and expense-account executives pretending to be gentlemen. Still, they're sitting ducks for private practice, which helps pay for the booze.'

'Your conscience is obviously in accord with the French doctor–novelist Céline. "The medical is an invidious profession. When one's practice is among the rich one looks like a lackey, when it's among the poor like a thief".'

'Putting it a bit strong, surely?'

'We don't think so in the Socialist Medical Association.'

'What's the odds?' I counter-attacked. 'My private patients have so little wrong with them they don't need a real doctor at all. They could easily be fobbed off on a mere psychiatrist.'

'We don't think that, either, in the Royal Academy of Psychiatrists. Of which I happen to be the Principal.'

The party was getting noisier.

'May a moth flap her wings round an old flame?'

I spun round, seizing both her hands. 'Margaret! Haven't changed a bit. I swear, you've got exactly the same number of freckles.'

That impish smile! 'You should know, Richard. Remember how you got me alone to count them, for some terribly important dermatological research you claimed to be doing?'

'*Didn't* we have fun?' I asked fondly. 'But hospitals *are* fun, they're not sickly gloomy places at all, because everyone is under thirty except the consultants, who anyway go home at teatime.'

'Well, yes, so long as you're not a patient in one, of course.'

'That torrid afternoon in the linen cupboard!' We both giggled. 'You know, if sister hadn't unexpectedly wanted a drawsheet, I'd have asked you to marry me.'

'I know, dear Richard.' She made a little kissing pout. 'Who *did* you marry in the end?'

'Over there, talking to Toby Hatchett, with the Campari and snub nose.'

'Oh, really? Fancy that. I'd hardly recognize her as that saucy staff nurse on orthopaedics.'

'Just think what you missed, Margaret!' I felt I expressed the wistful enchantment of dried wild flowers, some lovely claret past its prime, the recordings of dead virtuosi. 'You'd have enjoyed a delightfully contented life, wife to a respected GP in a cosy provincial town. Why, by now you'd be invited to the mayor's annual sherry party. You married Drippy Drawbell, didn't you?' She nodded. 'What's he up to now?'

'Oh, still going on being the Queen's physician.'

'Ah, Rollo, cheers.' I grabbed him passing. 'This'll be tough on my patients tomorrow. Remember the Stephen Leacock classic *How to be a Doctor*? "If the doctor has spent the night before at a little gathering of medical friends, he is very apt to forbid the patient to touch alcohol in any shape, and to dismiss the subject with great severity." But at the end of a long surgery, he tells the patient to drink whatever he can lay hands on, while "his eye glistens with the pure love of his profession".'

'I fancy that perceptive comment applies to much that we advise our patients. You know Lord Randolph, don't you?'

'Randy Randolph!' He was thin, pink, bald, shiny, long-whiskered, pop-eyed, like a dark-suited prawn. 'It must be fun, airing your views on medicine and having it all written up in *The Times* the next morning. For life, too, none of that squalid squabbling of being re-elected.'

'The first bitter political pill a doctor swallows' – even Randy's voice had a crustacean chill – 'is the realization that his profession is *not* of overwhelming, but of comparatively minor, importance in our national life.'

It was irresistible, digging him in the ribs. 'Remember when you were the prof's houseman, Randy? That nurse on your ward we called Linda the Last Minstrel, because she was such a terrific lay. I believe the whole hospital went through her.'

'Indeed, I do. Here's Lady Randolph with my drink. Thank you, Linda.'

'I think my wife's feet hurt.'

23 MAY

Sunday. Jilly appeared on Honda with laundry. I asked (routinely) if working hard. Replied disconsolately, no alternative, male students at St Botolph's as much use as celibate brotherhood of homosexual eunuchs. Startled. Not like my days, we considered by all females in hospital as pack of sexual beavers. Jilly explains. The most lusty students capitalize on masculinity by donating, for handsome fee, specimens of sperm for artificial insemination, at discreet clinic off Harley Street known throughout medical school as 'The Wank Bank'. All buying cars, video, polaroid cameras, etc., have no energies left for recreational purposes. Shocking state of affairs, I agree with her. Horrifying thought, St Botolph's students reproduced in limitless numbers all over country, like cloned Hitlers in that novel, also terrible fright of student doing obstetrics and at moment of delivery coming face-to-face with self, pure Edgar Allen Poe. As S J Perelman said in New York, 'De gustibus ain't what dey used to be.'

24 MAY

Mrs Astley, forty-four, non-smoker, wife of low-grade British Rail employee, shares semi-det on council estate with daughter, who is twenty-one, married to loader at local printing works and has baby aged six months. Mrs Astley slim, bright, embodies brains, drive, orderliness of family (as many working-class wives do, social fact mysteriously under-used by politicians).

Since Easter, complains shortness of breath hampers housework, shopping, pushing out grandchild, stairs killing her. Referred her to Dr Barty-Howells, new consultant physician at the General, everyone says brilliant.

Mrs Astley appears this morning, also opinion from Dr Barty-Howells, consisting strip light-blue paper printed:

FEV_1	1100
FVC	1540
FEV_1/FVC	71.4%
T_LCO	14.1
V (ALV)	2.61
K_{CO}	5.40

All as incomprehensible to me as mathematical formulae for stress on bridges, analysis oil-bearing rock, breakdown of supermarket sales, etc. Only guidance, further printout: K_{CO}: GREATER THAN PREDICTED BUT LUNG FUNCTION WITHIN NORMAL LIMITS.

Fine. Medicine gone totally scientific, everyone really a test-tube, interacting atoms now fully understood to cause digestion, peeing, pregnancy, hilarity, itching, spots before eyes, etc. All very well for high-class computerized specialists in ivory labs, but poor bloody GPs have the flesh-and-blood sitting opposite in M & S cardie with shopping, nervously awaiting few words which can alter entire life.

Feel like citizen struggling make ends meet, reading vapid effusions of economists on comfortable salaries, and just as unreliable. Told Mrs Astley to reverse arrangements in house, by which daughter had occupied ground floor because of baby. Also, prescribed her bottle of useless medicine.

Recall this happened before Christmas with Mr Patcham, council dustman, had bellyaches, received similar guidance: BILIRUBIN 12 MICROMOL/L THYMOL TUBIDITY 3 UNITS THYMOL FLOCCULATION 0.5 UNITS ZINC SULPHATE TURBIDITY 4 UNITS. Phoned Windrush, pathologist at the General, saying he could as usefully have sent fat stock prices, or tidal predictions at Dover. Windrush with usual medical-student humour said hoped horse well which pulled my carriage, presumed wore top-hat, frock-coat and spats, had I seen much of Lord Lister recently? No, presumably I was too busy cutting for stone, administering clysters, applying leeches. He had sent Mr Patcham's routine liver function tests, which were normal, should be jolly pleased. I told Mr Patcham to avoid chips, and cured him.

27 MAY

Telephone rang at half past midnight.

'Hello? Dr Gordon here.'

Deep groan.

'Hello? Hello?'

Groan now sepulchral. Concerned. Has patient just struggled to phone, exhausted strength dialling, expiring by British Telecom?

'Who is it, please?'

'This is…Damian Havers.'

Bolt upright in bed. 'Sir Damian! What a great pleasure to hear from you. I mean, not under the circumstances, of course. What's…what's the matter?'

'I am gravely ill.'

'I say, I'm dreadfully sorry.'

That voice! Unmistakable even *in extremis*. It continued with sacramental solemnity, 'I fancy I am in terminal anguish.'

'But what a terrible thing for the theatre. For you too, of course.' Why do I always become conversationally butter-fingered in presence of great actor, even over the phone? 'I'll be across just as fast as I can.'

A click. The rest was silence.

'What was it?' murmured Sandra dozily, as I jumped from bed. Told her. 'Oh, him! He'll overact playing the lead in his own funeral.' Went to sleep again.

Grab golf trousers, polo-necked sweater, collect bag from surgery, calm down Galen's barking, start car. Warm starlit night. Sir Damian's house 'Buskins' five miles south of Churchford, extensive views Weald of Kent. Elizabethan, lights ablaze in all leaded windows, pull ring beside oak door, bell clangs as on Inchcape Rock.

Long wait. Thin, pale, furrowed, gingery youngish man in jeans and denim top. Asks rudely, 'Yes?'

'It's Dr Gordon. You sent for me.'

'Oh, Christ, did she?'

'She?'

'You'd better go upstairs, I suppose. First right, past the loo,' he indicated with a languid flick. 'I don't know *what's* going on tonight, I really *don't*.'

He disappeared through a downstairs door, walking as though on a tightrope.

Upstairs. Light on, door ajar. Tap gently. Silence. Sidle inside, heart skips beat. Great actor perhaps already made final exit? Four-poster bed, gold-threaded coverlet, propped on pink pillows that silvery head, that famous pallid, long-jawed face so generously upholstered with eyebrow. He lay in beatific repose of nobleman reclining in saintly stone within an English church.

Lids jerked open on gleaming eyes, like pair of spotlights.

'Who is that?'

'Sir Damian, I was afraid I might be late. I was afraid just now I might be *too* late. There's no traffic in the wee hours of the morning, but your lovely house is at the end of so many confusing and twisting country roads, none of them apparently on any map –'

'*Who is that?*' Hollow-voiced, like the echo of some vast granite cave.

'It's the doctor,' I said reverently.

'I do remember an apothecary,
And Hereabouts 'a dwells, which late I noted in
Tatt'red weeds, with overwhelming brows
Culling of simples.'

He shut his eyes again.

'I saw your Romeo at Stratford,' I told him breathlessly. 'A memorable experience. Your mellifluous voice – how did the Sunday papers put it? Filling the theatre like some purple cloud smelling of hyacinths. What's the trouble?'

'I am dying.'

'So you said over the phone. But of what, exactly?'

He jerked up, left hand to breast, right towards the wealth of oak beams overhead.

'What, is Brutus sick,
And will he steal out of his wholesome bed,
To dare the vile contagion of the night
And tempt the rheumy and unpurged air...'

'Ah, Herbert!' The gingery man from downstairs advanced delicately into the room. 'Tell the doctor what happened.'

'She came over queasy after dinner,' he remarked with severe distaste.

'She? Who?'

'Sir Damian did.'

'Oh, I see. Yes. Well. It takes all sorts.'

'All sorts?' Sir Damian swivelled the spotlights. 'What do you *mean*, Doctor?'

'All sorts to...make the world.'

Herbert giggled. 'She'd make the world if she could, believe you me.'

'All the world's a stage,' began Sir Damian, 'And all the men and women merely players—'

'Oh, do shut up, duckie,' said Herbert.

'I'd better examine the abdomen.' I eyed the lilac silk pyjamas. 'If you'd, er, raise the curtain.'

Herbert fussed, pulling down bedclothes, undoing buttons. 'I *told* you, darling,' he scolded, 'you should have put on clean jamas for the doctor, these are *quite* a disgrace, not fit to be seen on a touring company chorus boy.'

Sir Damian jovially slapped the yellowish mole-spattered abdominal skin. 'In fair round belly with good capon lined, eh, Dr Gordon?' he resumed his speech.

I complimented him, 'You have a remarkably trim figure for a man of your age.'

He glared, as Richard the Third upon the lack of horses. 'Age? *Age?* How old do you think I am?'

'She's dreadfully touchy about her years,' Herbert said wearily. 'Ever since she had her face-lift.'

'I'd say you were in the first flush of, um, the prime of life.' I quickly felt his belly. 'The queasiness was nothing serious, I'm glad to say.'

He coughed, grabbing the sleeve of my tweed jacket, eye rolling in fine frenzy. 'The *death rattle!*'

'On the contrary, a frog in the throat.' I busied myself with my stethoscope. 'No cause for alarm. I can leave you some tablets.'

'Throw physic to the dogs.'

'Yes, Sir Damian, I saw your Macbeth, too, you were utterly spine-chilling with Banquo's ghost.'

'We opened in that in Leicester, didn't we, Herbert?' he observed. 'When the flat fell over in the middle of Act Three.'

'That's right, dear, you *would* wear that *dreadful* red wig.'

'The wig was a mistake.'

'Leicester was the cockroaches.'

'Was it? I thought Sunderland was the cockroaches?'

'Sunderland was that *ghastly* woman who quite *shamelessly* had a fit in the stalls, utterly *ruined* your dagger speech.'

I had something I was determined to say. 'You know, Sir Damian, it's wonderful to meet you in the flesh, as it were. I'm a tremendous theatre buff, have been ever since I was a student at St Botolph's, touring the annual panto round the wards. With the old joanna, and a barrel of beer on a stretcher, everyone falling about with laughter. The cast, that is, the audience were those patients too ill to let home for Christmas dinner. Though the ward sisters thoughtfully wheeled any at death's actual door into side-rooms, so they wouldn't ruin the performance by snuffing it before the interval. As one of the actors was always in the ward sluice-room being sick, and several more passed out before the end of the run, I learnt the art of ad-libbing, valuable onstage and off, I'd say…wouldn't you say…Sir Damian…?'

'I think I would like a bottle of champagne.'

'Champagne?' objected Herbert shrilly. 'I've never heard of such a thing.'

'Be a sweetie, go down to the green room and fetch me a bottle of the Bollinger.'

'Shan't. You'll be utterly pissed after all you managed to soak up at dinner.'

'You can be very cruel, Herbert.'

'*Somebody's* got to look after you, love, or you'd have been in a home, years ago.'

'I forgive you, Herbert.' Sir Damian instantly entered the last stages of feebleness. 'I should not on my deathbed care to breathe a bitter word, cherish an unkindly thought, about a poor player that has strutted and fretted his hour upon the stage...*with me.*'

'Oh, go on, with you,' said Herbert emotionally, 'it makes me want to cry.'

'Goodnight, sweet Herbert.'

'Oh, Damian...me old darling...' Herbert was on his knees at the bedside, eyes shimmering. 'Don't leave us yet. There's so many lovely things still left in life. They'll *have* to give you an Oscar one day, won't they? If you keep trying as hard as you do.'

'Ah, Doctor. You still here?'

Both stared. To break an awkward silence, I enquired, 'Have you ever played at Wyndham's Theatre, Sir Damian? You see, Sir Charles Wyndham was a doctor, one of the few to go on the boards. That was his stage name, of course, but "Colverwell's" wouldn't sound too exciting, would it?'

'I fancy that I could enjoy a digestive biscuit, Herbert.'

'There you go!' Herbert jumped up. 'Always asking for something we haven't got. Last week it was Mademoiselle Dior.'

'I've often thought, Sir Damian,' I persisted, 'there's a lot theatrical about medicine. I mean, we doctors have our patter, our stage gestures. We have our stars, not at all averse to applause. There's the costume of green gowns and masks, the lights, the girls, the items on the programme, though of course in *our* hospital drama it's real blood hitting the theatre ceiling. And in medicine, as on the stage, it's got to be all right on the night. No wonder Equity headquarters is at No. 8 Harley Street.'

'I shall get some sleep that knits up the ravell'd sleeve of care.'

'I should, duckie,' Herbert advised. 'You know you look an absolute wreck after lunchtime without your eight hours' beauty rest.'

'No further service, Doctor, until I send for thee.'

'What's that from, Sir Damian?'

'*Cymbeline,*' he told me. 'The Queen.'

77

'I know you're very tired, and not feeling at your best, but...might I...could I ask you for... I'm afraid I only seem to have an NHS form FP1O...your autograph?'

'*Of course*, dear boy. Perhaps you did not know that an act-*or*, a true act-*or*, would sign autographs for his undertaker? Do send your bill, though as I'm off for two years in Hollywood tomorrow, it might be a teeny while before it's paid.'

28 MAY

Another Bank Holiday weekend upon us. Mrs Astley appeared, completely recovered. What a wonderful vocation medicine is. It can triumph even over science.

JUNE

1 JUNE

'Ms Chairperson —'

At St Alphege's parish hall. Seven-thirty in the evening. On stackable plastic chairs, about sixty ladies, age-distribution balanced either side of menopause. Correct forms of address always tricky in England (what call Married Daughters of Viscounts, Eldest Sons of Earls in Holy Orders, Widows of Baronets Re-marrying, etc?). Now doubly so as groups so touchy, such as gays, criminals, immigrants, women.

'I am delighted to address the Persons' Institute on first aid.'

Not delighted at all. Stand nervously on stage where Gilbert and Sullivan sung at Christmas with same regularity as the carols. Trestle table, water carafe and Ms Buckingham-Smith, who runs everything, looks like Alice's Red Queen and just as prickly.

Vicar talked me into it, however much protested was prostituting myself, lecture could be given by St John's Ambulanceman, Boy Scout, swimming-bath attendant. Vicar said be realistic, no middle-class Englishwoman can possibly be lectured to by her social inferior, particularly as intimate parts of body liable to be mentioned.

'First aid is a subject of which it is essential we should all have a little knowledge. Nothing in everyday life is so gratifying as coming across a really serious street accident and pushing through the gawpers with the crisp information that I am trained to handle situations like this.'

'?'

'I have been doing exactly that since my first year's medical studies, which are restricted to the frog, dogfish and photosynthesis of plants. My honest belief that I could save a man's life once made me shoulder aside some old buffer fumbling with a tourniquet, as I told him, "You'd better let me tie that, grandad, *I am a medical student*." '

'!'

'He replied, quite politely, "Yes, I generally *do* leave them to handle this sort of thing, I'm the professor of surgery." '

'Ha, ha.'

Relieved.

As Hippocrates aphorized, 'The physician must have at his command a ready wit, as dourness is repulsive to the healthy and the sick.' But Churchford Women's Institute an audience to daunt the Marx Brothers juggling on one-wheel cycles.

'Thank you.' Offer theoretical background. 'First aid was invented by the Prophet Elisha who in the Second Book of Kings, "Put his mouth upon his mouth," and successfully gave the kiss of life to an apparently dead child. Very interesting, don't you think?'

' '

'Let's go on to something else.' Practical application always more gripping. 'Many people, of course, faint at the sight of blood. So you may discover someone bleeding to death in the roadway, with others going down like ninepins all over the pavements. Perform the major operation first. Bleeding can be stopped very simply by applying pressure with the fingertips to certain specific points of the body. If I may have a volunteer –? Ah, Mrs Blessington, our local tennis champion.'

Not noticed her in blur of audience. Blonde, cornflower eyes, ripe strawberry lips, preserved in the eternal thirties like some beautiful, lithe snow-leopard in the permafrost. Entrancing figure, bosoms symmetrical as milk jellies from same mould, wears Harrods undies (a patient). Do not even dare indulge fantasies about her, as fear somehow General Medical Council will get to know of it.

'*Hello*, Doctor.' Mrs Blessington mounts stage.

Adopt professional face. 'Pressure just here in the neck stops bleeding from the head.'

Push two fingers above gently moving clavicles, trying to preserve relationship of Smithfield meat inspector to side of beef. Raise Mrs Blessington's right wrist to horizontal, no resistance, on the contrary.

'Here in the armpit stops bleeding from the arm.' Take deep breath, clear throat. 'And here in the groin stops bleeding from the leg *thankyou* Mrs Blessington.'

'See you at the Noakes' cocktail party Saturday week, Doctor?'

'Possibly, possibly…'

'I *do* hope so, Doctor. We country girls of Churchford fall flat for such charm over the canapés.'

'Always busy, you know. There's a lot of it about this time of year.'

'*Do* make an effort, Doctor.' Inviting smile. 'Just to please *me*.'

She kindly leaves the stage. Audience now looking at lecturer with keen interest.

'Bandaging. When I was a student at St Botolph's Hospital, bandaging was zealously studied by the nurses, as something which made it obvious they were treating the patient. Many people were so enthusiastically bandaged they looked like Egyptian mummies. Indeed, several died before they could be unwrapped to find out. Our nurses could do spicas, capelines, reversed spirals, figures-of-eight, the gauntlet and demigauntlet, suspensory and many-tailed – lovely names, aren't they, like the steps in "Come Dancing". The doctors, of course, let the bandages fly about like rolls of loo paper from the football terraces, just to show they were as superior to such arts as to skivvying. Yes, Mrs Blessington?'

'I'd just like everybody to know, Doctor, that you took such care putting a super bandage up my thigh for my hamstrings.'

'Now for the Steak House Syndrome –'

'You had me on the court again within a month.'

'Delighted all went so well, Mrs Blessington –'

'I'm sure only because you insisted on retying it every other day for a whole fortnight.'

'The Steak House Syndrome. I expect you've all heard about that?' Mrs Blessington sat down, thank God. 'Imagine the scene. A diner is chomping his way through his T-bone rare, a gristly bit goes down the wrong way, he turns blue in the face and passes away in soundless asphyxiation. It's called "the silent coronary", I suppose, among steak buffs. Only the most churlish management would present his table with the bill.'

'????'

'In my days as a keen young houseman, I came across this emergency quite often, the food in hospital being uneatable. I would leap up with a scatter of French fries and crispy onions, demand a sharp, pointed knife from the kitchen, double clean tablecloth over my arm for sterility, and prepare to make a life-giving nick in the neck. Actually, whenever the victim saw me approach like a matador, he gasped with terror and projected the tit-bit like the cork from a bottle of badly chilled champagne. Nowadays, such dramatics are unnecessary, we doctors have a special manoeuvre, which I'd like to demonstrate – ah, Mrs Blessington again.'

'I'm sure this is something *very* important for all of us to know,' she said solemnly.

'Absolutely. Very. Most. Now er, would you kindly turn round, facing the hall? I shall stand close behind you, like this, see. Could you please stay completely still? Thank you. Now I clasp my hands tight round your midriff from behind and squeeeeeeeeze. All right?'

'I must go to more steak houses, Doctor.'

'Let us discuss shock – '

'That all, Doctor?'

'Yes. All. Totally. Thank you, Mrs Blessington.'

'Thank *you*, Doctor.'

'Let us discuss shock. You tender-hearted persons from persons' institutes throughout the land regard the cure for shock as a nice cup of tea. If they drop the bomb, I'm sure you'll all be ready and alert behind your urns. But shock is to we doctors – yes, Mrs Blessington?'

'I wondered if you were going to give us resuscitation of the apparently drowned, Doctor?'

'Naturally. No first aid lecture would be complete without resuscitation of the apparently drowned, no more than the *Folies Bergère* without the can-can. Using Shafer's method – '

'But *Doctor*,' Mrs Blessington chided gently. 'That's as out of date as a tennis-racket press.'

'Oh, is it? I wouldn't know, because I never go on the beach in summer, I mean that would be like a butcher taking his holidays in a meatworks.'

'Absolutely everyone now uses the Holger Nielsen method. It's called after the Danish army officer who invented it.'

'Of course.'

'May I demonstrate? I'm sure you'd like to see, fellow members?' Mrs Blessington was on stage. 'Just lie on the floor, Doctor. That's right, face down. Let your head go completely slack in my hands, so I can turn it to one side. No splinters, I hope? Now, I come in front of your head like this…one knee by your left ear…the other foot by your right one. I *would* be wearing a tight skirt today, wouldn't I? I don't suppose you'd mind keeping that position for a little while? Watch, everyone. I place my hands flat over the doctor's shoulders – Doctor *do* relax, it's like trying to do it with a giant panda. Now comes the vital bit. I rock forward, so, the weight of my body forcing air from your lungs –'

'Ouch!'

'Something the matter, Doctor?'

Dying. Croak, 'Can't breathe! Can't breathe!'

'Then I'll give you the kiss of life. Just turn over –'

Terrible pain. 'You've bloody well fractured a rib!'

'Have I? Oh, awfully sorry,' she apologized, like the Old Man of the Sea astride Sinbad. 'But really that's no more than a string going in your racket, is it? Doctor, don't panic! You know we first-aiders positively *enjoy* tackling an emergency.'

'Yes, like the fire brigade manned by a bunch of arsonists,' I spluttered. 'Ms Chairperson! This isn't all-in wrestling on the telly, for God's sake get someone to dial 999 and rush me to hospital. *And* see they bleep no one but a fellow of the Royal College of Surgeons.'

Lie on floor, barely breathing, hardly moving, all had abandoned plastic chairs, crowding round footlights, staring intently.

I suppose if you prostitute yourself you must expect to get fucked, as Hippocrates should have said.

2 JUNE

Receive jokey card with balloons, champagne corks, high-kicking girls saying IT'S PARTYTIME! The Noakes, Saturday after next. As Mrs Blessington going, no alternative but brusque refusal.

Not fractured rib, in fact ambulance crew shirty, as ran into parish hall with stretcher, oxygen, cardiac arrest equipment, had impression over phone of major disaster, probably roof fallen in, were within hair's breadth of inviting fire brigade along as well. Mollified them with price of few beers. Have extensive bruising upper thorax, explain to Sandra how incurred in embarrassing circumstances, she not sympathetic, says too old to play games with girls.

5 JUNE

Being Saturday, drive across to Maidencester races with major and our wives. Not racing man. Can understand even some of Windrush's pathology reports from the General, but find doubles and trebles, forecasts, accumulators, jackpots and Yankees as baffling as astrophysics. Major generously offers to 'mark my card', mentions he as shrewd judge of horseflesh as Queen's trainer, well-known fact in golf club. Lose every race. Major mystified. Says for years made handsome profit at Maidencester. I reply gloomily, no use cheering up dying patient by saying all other cases have recovered.

6 JUNE

Not yet sent refusal to Noakes, though impossible to go, and find self face-to-face with Mrs Blessington (more dignified than position of last confrontation, I suppose). Sunday, so no post, shall pen a brief excuse tomorrow.

7 JUNE

Seems hard on Noakes, cutting their party, blighting their social life just to avoid Mrs Blessington, who am still very cross with, as Samson with Delilah.

10 JUNE

Mrs Noakes herself at end morning surgery.

'Doctor! Thank God I've caught you!' Bursts free of receptionist's watchdog paws, slams door, throws self in patient's chair. 'Something terrible has happened.'

'Your husband? Locked in the sauna again? By an odd coincidence,' I reminisced with a chuckle, 'on the last occasion Sandra and I were having boiled beef for dinner—'

'My marriage. It's over. Utterly and finally.'

Sits hands dangling between pink, skin-tight South Molton Street trousers, expression like Anna Karenina enquiring time of next train. Pretty, green-eyed, chestnut hair in soft curls, figure boney, tits nothing like Mrs Blessington's.

'Not on a lovely morning like this?' I protested. (June! Strawberries, roses, long warm evenings stretching after work, doubling a man's days. Winter forgotten like nasty illness.) 'Your marriage usually breaks down in the flu and hypothermia season,' I pointed out.

'This time Hereward has gone too far, utterly too far. The sacrifices I've made for that man!' Hands clasping neck of Malaysian silk shirt, thin gold bracelets jingling. 'Cooking his dinner. Running his home. Tolerating his relations. Watching BBC2. Oh God! It's emotionally unbearable, have you any tissues?'

'These swabs do, Mrs Noakes?'

'Thank you.' She sniffed. 'I've made myself a complete martyr to his career. Complete! Those unending business dinners, at boring places like the Dorchester and the Savoy. I swear, I've cracked more lobster claws than I've shaken hands,' she complained piteously. 'He's always flying off somewhere, to New York, Tokyo, Sydney, and he thinks bringing me a few presents from Saks or the Ginza or King's Cross ample compensation for loyally sitting at home and carrying the *whole* burden of the household on my shoulders, remembering to send his suits to be valeted, getting people to clean the carpets, making sure there's someone in when Harrod's deliver. You can't imagine what backbreaking work it is running a home these days, I've had three different gardeners the past fortnight.'

I began sympathetically, 'The problem of the executive wife's loneliness – '

'Lonely? Me? I've far too much on my plate,' she told me shortly. 'I've hardly a moment even to see my manicurist – that's another thing Hereward said, a woman with time for a manicurist is living an unfulfilled life. I don't know *what* he meant, but he's always making obscure remarks, I think it's from watching "Call My Bluff".'

Mrs Noakes started to sob again. I made notes. Call pet shop for sack Galen's dehydrated dog food. The lawn *must* be mown after dinner, Sandra pick up can petrol from Straker's garage.

'Hereward' s always complaining he's perpetually roaming the world like the Flying Dutchman with a gold-blocked briefcase,' Mrs Noakes resumed, 'when he says he'd much rather be playing golf with his cronies here at Churchford. But *I* know the truth.'

'You do?'

'He only travels to get away from me.'

'Really? On what evidence?'

'Evidence? One doesn't need evidence with Hereward. One knows. Oh, Doctor – !'

'Run out of swabs? Try this varicose vein dressing.'

'You must think me a fool.'

'A weeping woman or a brave man can never be thought a fool.'

'Isn't that nice.' She sat back, crossing pink suede boots, smiling touchingly. 'You're so sympathetic, Doctor. So supportive.'

'As Lord Lister said,' I remarked modestly, ' "There is only one rule of practice, put yourself in the patient's place".'

'How I wish I was married to you instead of Hereward.'

'I don't think so, not really. You haven't seen me without my medicine-man's mask.'

'I'm sure a lot of women would love to be married to a doctor. Such understanding, down to the very *roots* of your soul. On tap day and night, like the bathwater.'

'It's not a wish generally expressed by my female patients,' I said guardedly.

'I'm sure they're all too shy, you should just *hear* some of the things they say when we talk about you in the hairdressers,' she continued disquietingly. 'You *are* coming on Saturday, of course?'

'But if your marriage has bust, you'll have to cancel Saturday, won't you?'

'Typical! Typical of Hereward. I've been looking forward to this party all summer, and entirely because of his own behaviour it's off. Can I hold your hand?'

'No more than I can hold the hand of the lovely lady who reads the nine o'clock news. Same principle. I think we'd better substitute consultation for conversation. How about what Masters and Johnson would call the plateau phase of your sexual response?' (As Freud said in 1893, 'The great majority of severe neuroses in women have their origin in the marriage bed.')

'Is that dressing soaked?' I enquired. 'Use the crêpe bandage.'

'It's funny, Doctor, but – why, now I'm starting to giggle – Hereward and I are like the landing light switches. When one's turned on, the other's turned off, I feel enormously gentle and loving right after dinner. Food always has that effect on me. While Hereward is always snorting and lusting at midnight, when all I want is eight hours' sleep. After watching one of those utterly grabbing medical programmes on the box, I decided it was all the fault of our biorhythms, and wondered if Hereward and I should have operations to reset our internal clocks.'

'It would be simpler to reset your mealtimes.'

'That's out of the question. Fiametta and Ortrud would simply walk out of the house.'

Puzzled. Childless couple. Had all the tests. No hope. Sudden double adoption? Test-tube babies? Cat and dog?

'The *au pairs*,' Mrs Noakes explained. 'The struggle it is, keeping a reasonably comfortable home for your husband with those *ghastly* foreign girls. *Why* other countries never teach their school-children English I don't understand, as I can't speak a word of their languages. We've had so many of them coming and going, the house sometimes resembles Victoria Station in August. They're all lazy and stupid, but that's only what you'd expect. The French sneer at the food as though it was leftovers from a swill-bucket, the Swedes are sex-mad even with the postman, the Dutch eat cheese for breakfast, if you can imagine it, the Italians must have been in the Mafia Girl Guides, the Finns are perpetually in tears and the Germans are still behaving as though they'd won the war. It's intolerable. I'm going to have another little cry.'

'Perhaps we'd better break open this pack of disposable baby's nappies.'

'Fiametta and Ortrud are quite the worse we've ever had, *and* they seem to think they're in the house as our equals, perfectly infuriating, but I suppose it's inevitable with the EEC. Fiametta's a plump Italian with bubble curls and enormous brown eyes, Ortrud's from Hamburg, six feet tall with blonde plaits, she can squeeze a grapefruit one-handed. Both are having the most torrid affair with Hereward, it's perfectly obscene.'

'Sounds as though he might have his hands full, particularly with that sciatica.'

'They're always leaving the bathroom unlocked deliberately for him to stumble in, or screaming round in their nighties because of burglars, and walking about almost stark naked when he's practising his putting on the lawn. Naturally, Hereward denies violently there's the slightest thing between them. You know why?'

'Perhaps because there isn't?'

'No, it's only to refuse me the satisfaction of feeling jealous. He's continually trying to avert my gaze from the ruins of our marriage by dragging me to Glyndebourne or Wimbledon or Lord's or such places where executives are obliged to go and drink champagne with their clients. Now do you see what a martyr I am?'

The telephone rang on my desk.

'Excuse me…hello, Dr Gordon speaking. Yes, she is, as a matter of fact…no, you're not disturbing anything in the slightest intimate… I'll tell her. Bye. That was Hereward,' I informed Mrs Noakes.

'Oh? Didn't he want to try wheedling me?'

'No, he just phoned to say he'd arrived at his office in the City to find his firm's got a couple of tickets for Ascot next week.'

'He can't get round me like that.'

'Royal Enclosure.'

'Oh, God, I've hardly a thing to wear.'

11 JUNE

Still undecided about Noakes tomorrow. Mention problem to Sandra (carefully, as if utterly trivial matter). She says couldn't care less, had I forgotten Saturday night her St Botolph's Nursing School reunion at Café Royal, I shall have to endure meeting adoring female patients socially on my own. Decide best all round if I go, phone at once.

12 JUNE

'Why, it's Mrs Blessington. Frightfully noisy cocktail party, isn't it?'

The Noakes' neo-Georgian house ('Shangri La' with gold bath-taps) lounge packed, liable to overflow through wide-open double-glazed patio doors into pool.

'*Hello*, Doctor. But why don't you call me Valerie? You can't wear your stethoscope all the time.'

'Right-ho, Valerie. How's your husband's gout?'

'I hear you're dreadfully, dreadfully angry with me.'

'What? You? Me? Ridiculous. Whatever for?'

'Mavis Buckingham-Smith said because I'd utterly ruined your lovely lecture, and crippled you for life into the bargain.'

'Oh, that? Completely forgotten about it, actually. Livened the evening up, if anything.'

'Will you tell me something, Doctor?'

'If it's within my professional competence.'

'It's puzzled me for ages, when you see a lovely lady lying on your couch, don't you get the *teeniest* sexy feelings?'

'How's your husband's gout?'

'Jim's just Concorded off to Washington for a week. You can imagine, my bed feels absolutely huge all night.'

'Gout is a most interesting condition, being strongly familial. I'm fascinated by genetics. Read a book about it. Incredibly complicated, it makes computer programming look like a knitting pattern. Perhaps I can explain, every human being possesses twenty-three pairs of chromosomes, each consisting of two identical chromatids, joined at the centromere—'

'I think I should feel *awfully* insulted, Doctor, if you didn't feel *some* stirrings.'

'There are three types of chromosomes, the metacentric, the submetacentric—'

'You *are* being coy, for a man who's seen more bare boobs than the Swedes open sandwiches.'

'If you must know, yes, I do.' Took third gin and ton from small dark girl resembling teenage Sophia Loren, assume Fiametta. Why not bare soul? 'After all, Valerie. I'm a medic, not a eunuch. But we doctors are trained to achieve sexual schizophrenia, to split our professional and private personality. The most voluptuous curves under our very eyes incite us no more than a picture postcard of the Taj Mahal.'

Mrs Blessington sighed across her *crème de menthe frappée*. 'Oh dear. *What* a waste of the Madame Rochas I always put on for you, Doctor. Just brushing a crisp from your lapel…'

'Did I hear you are a doctor? Well, fancy. I'm Nesta Smedley.'

Eager-faced gingery woman in crimson kaftan. Know only few guests – Chris (in advertising), awful new patients with the Rolls, the major, of course – assume most Hereward Noakes' clients, whom he obliged pass his days drinking with to earn living.

'You're going to be absolutely fascinated by my case,' Nesta Smedley assured me. 'It's my pelvis. It all started five years ago, when we were on holiday in Palma…'

'Evening, Hereward,' I exclaimed. 'Lovely party. Thanks, I'll take another gin and ton off you. Jim Humbles the town clerk over there is driving me home.' (Yesterday morning had conveniently put him off alcohol for a month.)

'Doc, I've got to talk to you about my stress.' Hereward, fair, tall, burly, Fifth Avenue silk suit. 'Running a financial consultancy these days is driving me into an early grave.'

'Stress and strain never killed anyone, my dear chap,' I told him zestfully. 'After all, you can't get more of either than by running a country or running a war, can you? Well, Churchill lived to ninety,' I reminded him. 'Eisenhower to seventy-eight, Adenauer to ninety-one, de Gaulle to seventy-eight and Mr Macmillan is the spryest of senior octogenarians. Of course, politicians are always moaning about the crushing cares of office, but pop stars are always moaning about being mobbed by their fans.'

'Doctor! You haven't listened to a word I've been saying about my pelvis—'

'Indeed, I have, Mrs Smedley. I'm sure it must have been dreadfully embarrassing, particularly through an interpreter.'

'But it was nothing, compared with two years later, when we were on holiday in Tunis...'

'Then what should I do, Doc, about feeling dead beat in the afternoons?'

'Drink a pint of water, Hereward.'

'With my lunch?'

'Instead of.'

'So I had the operation, at the London Clinic, naturally, and the surgeons all said it was quite the nastiest they'd ever seen...'

'Anything you say, Doc, though you've probably indirectly fired half my staff by next Monday teatime. Who advises on your financial affairs?'

'Oh, Sandra. The Abbey National and National Savings, you know.'

He was shocked. 'You mean, you haven't got *anyone*?'

'I play golf with the bank manager.'

'High Street banks are the whelk stalls of the financial world,' he announced scathingly. 'With sound advice from someone in the know — someone like me — you can make a lot of money, even these days.'

'Really?' Suddenly more interested. 'Perhaps if you've a spare moment—'

'It would be a real pleasure, acting for you, Doc.'

'*There* you are, Doctor!' Mrs Noakes, black velvet gold-spangled flying suit, Bloody Mary. She lovingly squeezed arm round husband. '*Now* I know what was wrong with me, and you didn't. Premenstrual tension!' she announced triumphantly.

'There's a lot of it about this time of – '

Hereward said, 'Women have just discovered it, like the sewing-machine.'

'Hereward, you *are* a bastard.' She kissed him fondly. 'You know perfectly well I have it every day of the year.'

Reflected Noakes marriage probably sounder than most in room. Executive classes tend to exhaustion through board meetings, jet lag, expense accounts, office politics, office parties, most inclined to follow advice of Dr Quesnay to Louis the Fifteenth – 'Ah! Sire! Change is the greatest aphrodisiac of all!'

'Hello again, Doctor! Just picking a cashew from your tie. Does it flatter you, if I say you're such a nice doctor?'

'It depresses me, Valerie. A President of the Royal College of Physicians once said that any fool can be a nice doctor, but it takes application and hard work to be a good one, which in the end is of more benefit to the patient.'

'What a silly president. Nothing makes you feel better than a nice bedside manner, no side effects either.'

'Perhaps a bedside manner works by suggestion,' I conceded. 'After all, politics, advertising and religion do.'

'Don't you find it boring, everyone cadging advice at a party instead of queuing for it in the surgery?'

'Terribly. But a man's doctor,' I told her virtuously, 'should be his friend in health, his ally in sickness and his companion in death. The middle's the difficult bit, so I do my best with the other two.'

'Just removing a cocktail onion from your collar. Tell me all about Helen Noakes' sex life.'

I was shocked. 'My dear Valerie! You're inviting me to break professional secrecy. A dreadful medical crime. Almost as bad as advertising for patients. I don't mind if I do,' I added, taking another gin and ton from a teenage Brünnhilde, presumably the grapefruit-squeezer.

Mrs Blessington observed, 'Doctor, you *do* get on your professional dignity, quite as naturally as politicians upon their soap-box.'

Nettled. 'We doctors don't make these rules to be pompous. Only to protect our patients.'

'But I'm always reading of medical records found in thousands on rubbish-tips, generally of embarrassingly famous bodies.'

'Slip-ups occur in the tightest security,' I said airily, recalling that a cabinet minister, hearing his psychiatrist's case notes blowing about Midlands dump, had instantly redirected load radioactive waste, shut area for thousand years.

'But Helen's absolutely desperate for sex when Hereward wants to watch the nine o'clock news, and when he's pawing the bedroom carpet like a randy rhino, she's snoring.'

Blanched. 'How did you know that?'

'Oh! everybody does. She's always talking about it in the hairdressers. You're awfully sweet, trying to be so deliciously diplomatic, *I* appreciate it even if she doesn't, in fact I esteem you more than any other man in Churchford, even if I *am* rather naughty when you're behaving like a guru.'

Stared. 'You do? Do you? Really?'

'I'm not at all like Helen Noakes, who puts on her personality like her eye-liner,' Mrs Blessington imparted intimately, 'mine is complicated and deep down, like those organs you *do* tend to go on about over dinner sometimes. Just extracting a cheese football from your cuff. If you'd care to pay a housecall…while Jim's in New York…it would be a *very* interesting one.'

'Valerie! Mrs Blessington! I mean, well, you know, it's enormously sweet of you. don't for one moment imagine that I'm not touched, flattered, made to feel instantly ten years younger, with a waistline and hardly noticeably bald at all, it's super for a man who imagines he's just wandering off into the prostatic twilight, and of course it would be utterly wonderful, I know that, I have sort of inspected the pitch, as it were, I do hope you don't mind a sporty metaphor, but unfortunately it's totally out of the question, absolutely, it's something far worse than case notes littering municipal dust-heaps, doctors don't, you understand, we simply cannot play fast and loose like ordinary chaps, I'm not being pompous, I'm not being dignified, I only wish dear Mrs Blessington, Valerie I mean, that was the only reason for spurning your lovely suggestion, but we doctors must stick to the rules, we must be either superhuman or struck off.'

'But doctor! I was only asking you to see my sister's family, who're keeping me company while Jim's away, her husband's from Tasmania, where apparently they have lots of those mixed-up chromosomes you're so interested in, and the kids have got twelve fingers each.'

'What shall I do about my pelvis now?'

'I advise you to consult a doctor, Mrs Smedley.'

'But you are one! Aren't you?'

'Of philosophy. But I still found it fascinating.'

Put down glass. Going. *Must* keep professional and private life apart, however difficult in normal man responding to what Jilly's Rimini dentist called *profumo di donna*. Grave danger being hauled before GMC, worse, look bloody fool. Feel gentle grope.

'Just taking a stuffed olive from your shirt-buttons, Doctor... Jim's Concording to Rio next month, when my sister's back in Australia. So...perhaps a naughty girl can make amends for sending up a lovely man? Mmmm, Doctor...? Mmmmmmmmm...? Care to see me out to my Merc?'

'Oh God. Why did I take up bloody medicine?'

14 JUNE

Hereward Noakes appears after evening surgery (privately, naturally). Worried about sciatica. Tell him could be due to all sorts of trouble in spine, which any specialist will feel obliged to start attacking, like Gas Board men with pneumatic drills. Pain mild, recommend masterly inactivity. Hereward health enthusiast, always jogging, weight-lifting, chest-expanding, probably puts on a track suit to have a fuck.

He says, came along also about financial health, Doctor, amazing what can gain by putting self in hands of professional, why, bulls, bears, stagging, take-overs, yield gap, cocoa futures, dawn raids, jobbers' turn, offshore funds, bed-and-breakfasting, all profitable if exploited by expert. Impressed. Hereward mentions, strictest confidence, Bald Coot Mine in Australian desert going up ten times in next fortnight, fabulous deposits, top secret report, how about as introductory offer, say a grand, his commission small percentage. Ask mine of what? He says maybe gold, perhaps copper, could be coal, financiers in City unconcerned with technical details, I feel ungrateful ignoramus, write cheque for thousand quid. He congratulates me on acumen, must say it seems an easier way of making money than peering down or up the various orifices of Churchford's population. Told Sandra we should shortly be rich, but she points out I have not yet even won anything on the Premium Bonds.

21 JUNE

Midsummer. Slack surgeries. Lovely. Before noon, phone call from Mrs Noakes, she utterly bedridden, could I please succour. Jump in car at once, round to 'Shangri La', up fully carpeted stairs to bedroom overlooking pool.

'The doctor so soon?' Smiles invitingly, throws aside *Harpers and Queen*. 'Advantage of being a private patient, I suppose? I was telling my daily woman only yesterday, *don't* dissipate your husband's wages on video and Horizon Tours and microwave ovens, join BUPA, *much* more rewarding.'

I am all professional (remember Mrs Blessington). 'How long have you been ill, Mrs Noakes?'

'I've been utterly prostrate all morning, do sit on the bed. These circular ones are rather fun. Just had the place refitted – Hereward asked rather grumpily why a bedroom had to match your lifestyle, when you were mostly unconscious in it – but when one's trapped here helplessly as I am today, one really appreciates one's Louis Quinze. Like the quilt? White goose down.'

'And what seems to be the trouble?' She in candy-striped trad nightshirt, unbuttoned all down front.

'My usual *intolerable* headache got worse and worse. Hereward wondered whether to stay at home, but of course I'd feel an utterly disloyal wife being ill and impeding his career, so I said, off you go in the

Jag, darling, I shall be a martyr – ah, Ortrud. What a gorgeous display from Moyses Stevens, Hereward must have got his secretary to order it just as soon as he reached the office, how caring of him. Where was I, Doctor – ? The damn phone never stops ringing, hello?'

Delightful smile. 'Fiona! How sweet to call me. Yes, I am, I'm afraid. *The doctor is with me now.*' Hushed solemnity. 'I hope it isn't *too* serious, either, but one never knows, *of course* I remember poor Janet Morgan-Jones, nothing but a slight cough and a week later that utterly freezing afternoon at the crematorium, thank you *so* much.'

Replaced pink telephone (little knobs instead of dial). 'Dreadful bitch, she only rang hoping I was half dead – oh, Fiametta. What a lovely basket of fruit. Why, it's from my fellow bridge-players, how thoughtful, I suppose they've taken enough money off me in my time. Peach, Doctor?'

'These headaches – how long have you had them?'

'Sometimes I think I was *born* with one.' Phone. 'Excuse me again. Hello? Pamela! Fiona just phoned you? Yes, the sad news is true, I'm in bed under the doctor. So we'll have to postpone our lovely lunch today until I'm completely fit, won't we? I know I've been overdoing it for months, I'd love to go somewhere and lie as flat as a haddock in the sun, but Hereward's desperately busy, and of course a top executive's wife is simply part of his job these days, a constant stream of Americans and Japanese and Arabs to be lavishly entertained, as soon as Mohammedans glimpse a bottle of Cliquot, all thoughts of reaching the Seventh Heaven fly from their minds. Bye! That's a date I don't mind missing, at that place Sylph's in Templar Lane, wonderful for our figures, shredded lettuce, grated celeriac and carrot juice, ugh. Have a chocolate, Doctor? They're *disastrous* for my weight, I know, but surely you can succumb to temptation when you're ill and feeling utterly awful?'

'Indeed, Mrs Noakes, *most* of my patients are martyrs to self-indulgence,' I remarked austerely. 'And who can blame them? Flu is the housewife's winter holiday. After being taken for granted all year, nothing makes mother more lovingly appreciated than the family coming home from work and having to cook its own mince and potatoes. Illness is a chance for most people to feel important, for many their only one. Do you know, I've seen patients in hospital as proud of their diseases as old soldiers of their scars.'

'It's all right for some,' Mrs Noakes objected, 'like my daily woman's husband, drawing their sick pay and lying reading the *Sun* all day, but I've always a million things to do. You should see my diary, coffee mornings for cystic fibrosis, hairdresser, garden centre, Oxfam – oh dear!' she remembered. 'I must phone Naomi and cancel our shopping expedition, though they're always so embarrassing, she's dreadfully broke, poor thing, her husband's only in middle management, I end up with something cheap and shoddy which is pure waste as I can't possibly be seen in it, not with Hereward, anyway.'

'About the headache –'

'Absolutely *throbbing*, right above the eyes. Yes, Ortrud? Ah, the portable Sony, put it beside the Teasmade, we usually let the *au pairs* have it, but I'd be stretched out here utterly bored, and I should *die* if I didn't see what happens next in *Crossroads.*'

'Any other symptoms, Mrs Noakes?'

'Doctor, I'm utterly *riddled* with them, sleeplessness, weariness, lassitude, complete loss of appetite – Ortrud, I'll just have an egg and milk beaten with brandy for lunch, I've got to keep my strength up, surely that's what Dr Gordon would advise?'

Ortrud retired to Nibelheim.

'Now she's gone, I can be utterly frank.' Mrs Noakes patted the bed beside her. 'Make yourself comfy with a pillow. Do you know what *I* think causes my headaches? My sex life with Hereward. I'll start right at the beginning, with my honeymoon – but I'm not the slightest feverish,' she objected.

'Thermometer under the tongue, please.' The doctor's oldest trick. 'It's a rather old-fashioned instrument, takes five minutes to work, ten if we want to be absolutely sure.'

Sat on bed and read *Vogue.*

'Thank you, Mrs Noakes.' Removed it. 'Perfectly normal. I'm sure that's a relief?'

'It's given me time to sort out exactly what I'm going to say –'

'And it's given me time to make a diagnosis,' I interrupted firmly. 'In 1901, Freud wrote *The Psychopathology of Everyday Life* — '

'*I* certainly have none of those awful complexes he described.'

'On the contrary, Mrs Noakes, every woman wears under her skirt a Freudian slip. The book was as popular with ordinary readers as with doctors, because people were fascinated by his idea that lots of highly irrational human behaviour was really highly rational. Getting on the wrong train and avoiding your creditors. Making a detour and missing an impudent beggar. Asking for the wrong number, of a girl you didn't dare to speak to — he was writing in the days before dialling and assertive sexual manners. Losing an umbrella, because you'd stolen it. Losing even your memory, to hide yourself like an ostrich in the desert. Ever suffered from amnesia, Mrs Noakes?'

'Well, if I had, it would be something I'd want to forget.'

'Do you know why you're spending today in bed?'

'Because of my headache.'

'No! You haven't got a headache. Or if you have, it's no worse than one you'd exorcise with an aspirin and then go off to Ascot or Henley. You're in bed because you don't want to consume raw veg with Pamela nor shop down-market with Naomi, you want to get your own back on the bridge club and savage the box of Suchard which has been the temptation of the Devil since your party, better still, to milk sympathy from your flinty-breathed friends, and better than that — !' I paused. 'Have your husband tell you he loves you with flowers.'

She stared silently at the fitted dressing-table unit. At last I was getting on top of Mrs Noakes. Professionally, that is. I asked intensely, 'What are you missing this evening?'

'A lovely birthday party at the Hyde Park Hotel for the son of Hereward's chairman. Then we were all going on to see *The Sound of Music.*'

'An unmarried son, I take it?'

'Yes.'

'Of course, Hereward will be present?'

'Yes.'

'Might I ask you something painful, Mrs Noakes?'

'Yes.'

'You'll be frank with me?'

'Yes.'

'This young man – what's his name –? '

'Robin.'

'Have you been out with him?'

'Yes.'

'I mean, by yourselves.'

'Yes. When Hereward's in New York or somewhere, and I'm lonely.'

'Ha! Where do you go?'

'Generally, I've driven up to London and had lunch with him.'

'Ha, ha! You're fond of him?'

'Yes. I am. Very.'

'Ha, ha, *ha*! And he of you?'

'Extremely, by all evidence.'

'There we are! Diagnosis made. You don't want to be in the simultaneous company of Hereward and Robin. Mrs Noakes, you are suffering not from headaches, but feelings of guilt.'

'I don't see why.'

'It's very flattering for any woman to invoke the attentions of a sexy young feller.'

'It is, Doctor, it is, but the chairman's son is only six.'

'Oh.'

She smiled. 'You're terribly sweet to take such trouble over my case, but you've got it wrong. My marriage, my social life, Hereward's job, they're the only things I've got to fuss over. If only I could have had a child…'

She held my hand. For once, I let her.

30 JUNE

Front page of *The Times*: BALD COOT CRASH SYDNEY POLICE HOLD DIRECTORS.

Telephoned Hereward's office. He cheerful, said couldn't understand why tip went wrong, he as shrewd judge of mines as veteran Forty-niner, well known fact in the City. Better luck next time, he laughs, let me see, how much did you invest? Spluttered, a thousand. Oh, well, no cause to lose sleep, then, he says, only a trivial sum down the drain, hopes I'll come for drinks with them Sunday morning.

With friends like Hereward and the major, who needs ruinous dissipations?

JULY

1 JULY

'The English winter – ending in July to recommence in August.' Byron got it right, at least until 8.30 a.m.

'Good morning, Mr Cowley. What a lovely day! Had your holiday yet?'

'No, Doctor, that's why I've come. You know how me and the wife are always careful over our health?'

'Of course. You wear crash helmets for your ride-on mower. Admirable.'

Mr Cowley, dark, neat, comfortable house overlooking Pilgrim's Way, runs office-supply business. Small, brown-haired wife subservient as a spaniel. Regular patient, in waiting-room plays musical chairs to avoid touch, breath, undefined miasmas from fellow-patients, gets on Mrs Shakespear's nerves. Gather from his wife that on return from surgery Mr Cowley immediately strips, has clothes laundered, takes bath, probably adds pint or two of Jeyes' Fluid. He would seem concerned about germs.

'Though of course, Doctor, this is the salubrious season –'

'Salubrious? You're joking. Haven't you thought about the perils of summer? Do you realize that wasps and bees claim five British lives a year? Which is more than you can accuse our atomic power-stations of, eh? Though I don't suppose there'd be much keenness for a demo round the hives. Ban the Bee and that sort of thing. You can be struck by lightning, nipped by adders, do a fry-up of toadstools, swig the weedkiller, spin off the rollercoaster, get beaten up by mods and rockers on the prom, not to mention everyday drowning and falling off cliffs. It's happening all season.

Plus tennis elbow, nettlerash, hay fever, poison ivy and midsummer madness.'

Overkill only way to treat his assumption whole world as dangerous as London 1664–5.

'But surely, Doctor,' Mr Cowley protested nervously, 'The lovely sunshine –'

' "The great bronze disc of church-emptying Apollo, hardener of heart and skin." ' Arms flung wide, quoting Cyril Connolly, obese man of letters. 'Sunlight absolutely wrecks the epidermis, though I suppose it can hardly be accused of fossilizing the coronaries.'

'I'm with you there,' he said more cheerfully. 'I always baste the wife with Ambre Solaire, and fold a fruit-gum packet for my nose.'

'When were you conceived?'

Looked blank. 'Beg pardon, Doctor?'

'Some interesting research was done in America ten years ago. You'd imagine summer was Nature's smiling season for starting babies, wouldn't you? Dancing round the maypole, plenty of cover in the cornfields, it's traditional.' He nodded obediently. 'But no,' I corrected him. 'Love in the winter produces, the following autumn, one-third more offspring with high IQs than summer's passion fruits. People like Picasso and Mrs Thatcher, as opposed to Mozart and Mr Macmillan.'

'Perhaps that's because clever people don't watch so much telly during the winter nights?' he suggested (I thought rather brightly).

'A professor in Dublin said it was the thunderstorms.'

'I know they turn the milk, Doctor, we always pour ours away just in case, though the man from Unigate says we're daft.'

'Thunderstorms cause anxiety in newly pregnant women, which mental state affects the hormones circulating in her blood, which in turn get through to the baby and blunt the cutting-edge of its brain.'

'A bit far-fetched, isn't it?' Mr Cowley complained morosely. 'Why only thunderstorms? It's really worrying, these days, the number of things there are to make you anxious.'

'The Dublin professor went further. He reckoned *whole countries* became anxious.'

'How'd he know?' Mr Cowley demanded.

'Easy. You go by the suicide rate, car smashes, alcoholism and so on. I don't know exactly *why* they should be barometers of anxiety, but the professors do. Japan is the most anxious country, with Italy and France. *All have lots of thunderstorms.* The first ear-splitting crack, the Japanese start committing *hara-kiri*, the French grab the cognac, and the Italians continue driving as usual. We in Britain are terribly lucky, because we have only a few thunderstorms and a placid, easy-going temperament. In the Dublin professor's own country, I shouldn't imagine it ever thunders at all. Where are you going for your hols?'

'That's where I wanted your advice, Doctor,' he replied eagerly. 'Travelling's always a health hazard, I reckon, even stopping for a pork pie at a motorway caff, never know what it can give you.'

'How right you are,' I agreed heartily. 'Millions of air passengers buzzing round the world, more pestilential than rat fleas. Nowadays, you needn't go all that way to the White Man's Grave to catch horrible tropical diseases, you can suffer them in the convenience of your own bedroom. We doctors see malaria in Muswell Hill, Lassa fever in Lyme Regis, typhus in Taplow and sleeping sickness in Slough.'

'The wife and I know that foreigners have some funny health habits, of course. Just like their other ones. We'd certainly not care to bathe from their beaches –'

'You no longer swim in the Mediterranean. You go through the motions. Old medical joke.'

'So we thought we'd be safer on a cruise.'

'Are you mad? Shut yourself in a tin can wallowing in the hot sun, everyone blowing germs over each other from the range of a few inches? Thousands of miles from the nearest life-support system? I exclude the lifeboats, of course.'

'But every cruise liner carries a qualified doctor –'

'Don't talk to *me* about ship's doctors. Their surgical skills are limited to splicing the mainbrace. I ought to know, because I was one. Ships are terribly dangerous places, Mr Cowley, take it from me. I'd have put icebergs as the least of the *Titanic*'s troubles.'

103

'Well, if we do risk going abroad, on terra firma, as you might say, can you recommend a country which provides a proper doctor, should anything go wrong?'

'A country's medicine has its own style, like its music,' I said romantically. 'In France, they tend to give everything by suppository, even cough mixture. In Spain, the whole family comes into hospital with you. In Brazil, you have to bring your own sandwiches. In Italy, people pray over you a good deal. In Germany, they have means of making you better. In America, all regular credit cards are accepted. A lot of British patients today could go to India and Pakistan, fall ill, and still feel at home,' I pointed out hearteningly. 'Why not .Japan? There's this new hotel in Osaka.'

'What's special about it?' he asked warily.

'It consists of 411 sleeping capsules, like a honeycomb. Burn a greenhouse fumigating cone, crawl inside, shut the lid, and you'll be free from infection for a fortnight. You can't even fall out of bed. Good morning.'

'Where are *you* going Doctor?'

'Nowhere. In this job, you never really feel fit enough to face a holiday.'

5 JULY

Monday morning, Mrs Shakespear off on hols (Isle of Wight), Sandra as usual takes over receptionist's desk. Mrs Shakespear seen by patients as dragon, to me highly sophisticated security system. Wonderful at scolding queue jumpers, humbling grand ladies, snubbing uppish socialists, defusing irate tories, frustrating waiting-room lawyers, comforting distressed mums, disarming children of water-pistols, calming excitable teenagers, silencing babies, rebuffing drug reps, giving general impression that seeing the doctor a privilege comparable with seeing the glory of God, and equally effective. She once had entire waiting-room in tears over my being called to a dying child in a caravan, though in fact playing golf with the major. Did Mrs S. run things instead of Mrs T., country would be contentedly buzzing busy hive.

Effect of Sandra on immediate circle same as replacement of Lucrezia Borgia by Florence Nightingale. Sandra naturally not so efficient, find self discussing coming baby with unmarried secretary, treatment of alcoholism with churchwarden, through muddle in record cards. Always terribly polite to Sandra about errors (only way), wonder how other professional couples have managed, the Curies, for instance.

8 JULY

This morning saw Mrs Charrington, headmistress of St Ursula's (fnd. 1920, 300 girls, boarding fees three thou plus a year, bright blue uniform, summer straw hats, Oxbridge successes, tennis and netball, careers mistress, gravel soil). She large, pink, jolly, in sensible non-crush grey linen suit, sensible 20-denier seal tights, sensible flat-heeled shoes, sensible brooch of Royal Navy Crest, and tiny red blisters all up her forearms.

Reassure her, 'It's a slight allergic rash, Mrs Charrington, there's a lot of it about this time of year.'

She affronted. 'But it's utterly amazing that I'm here at all, I always take such good care of my health, and of my girls' health at St Ursula's. I permit nothing in their school dinners grown with chemical fertilizers, what comes out of a factory is far less natural than what comes out of a horse, that's obvious.'

Mrs Charrington is a compost-grown-stone-ground-wholemeal-sunflower-oil nut.

'I always buy health foods, Doctor, at the Hygea Stores in Templar Lane, they're criminally pricey, but I'm sure *you'll* agree nothing's too much to pay for a *corpore sano*, even if a *mens sana* is utterly impossible to maintain these days. I've quite a reputation in the common room for my wholesome gourmet treats,' she revealed. 'You must come one evening for my sesame seed stew with mung beans, topped up with a dollop of halva on charcoal crackers.'

'I'll write you a prescription –'

'My husband George simply couldn't start the day without his muesli with tenderized prunes and a vegetable sausage – the poor man is an absolute martyr to the wind – and after my lunchtime slug of ginseng I can face the girls like a giant refreshed. I feed my husband on lots of living raw foods because he is, as you know, somewhat short and of thin physique, the fifth form scrawled some outrageously vulgar graffiti about him in the loo. I must confess, I visited the hakim's shop by the station – 'hakim' means 'wise one', you'd be called that in Bangladesh, Doctor – and bought George some powered rhino horn, which is famous over two continents for putting lead in pencils, as they say, this is in the *strictest* confidence, if the fifth form got to hear I don't know *what* I'd find in the loo.'

'I'll give you an antihistamine drug –'

'As I'm being jolly frank, I can tell you there were evenings during our courtship when I insisted George had a dozen oysters.'

'And only ten of them worked, I suppose? Old joke.'

She frowned. 'I don't follow, Doctor? And I'm famous at St Ursula's for my sense of humour.'

'Try it on the fifth form,' I advised.

'There's a lot you doctors can learn you know. George's poor back, doctors despaired of it, so he went to an osteopath, one crack and never a twinge since. My sister Pru had a lot of feminine trouble, the doctors were utterly hopeless, actually suggested a psychiatrist, quite insulting, my family are *perfectly* normal, she went to see a man in Pimlico who stuck foot-long needles all over her and cured her instantly. I remember he said that it let out her *qi*, the energy of life – I must say Pru has enough for a dozen, a dreadfully talkative woman – and that trouble was imbalance of her *yin* and *yang* which does sound rather like a team of Chinese acrobats. My other sister Crystal suffered from vertigo, she got converted to RC, so she made the pilgrimage to Lourdes, it was rather a disaster, she had a nasty attack in the sacred grotto and fell into the candles, they had to put her out by sluicing her with the holy water.'

'These tablets may cause sleepiness –'

'My brother Clarence suffered lassitude for years, quite baffled Harley Street, then he heard about radiesthesia, he sent them a few hairs to put in their black box and test for vibrations, they told him he'd got overstrain, though as a joke he'd sent hairs from the tail of his Labrador, he gave the dog some conditioning powders and from that day they both never looked back.'

'So be careful if you're driving –'

'Now I'm into, as the fifth form say, yoga, I stand George on his head every morning and I do my *asanas*, which are yogic postures, on my study floor during bun-break. I know you doctors don't approve of unorthodox medicine, no more than those dreadful trade unions their childish scabs and blacklegs, but *why* does it make the patients feel better?'

'A little of what you fancy does you good.'

'Heavens, is that the time?' She stared at her sensibly huge wristwatch. 'The lower sixth will become utterly Trotskyist if they're kept waiting. As I'm here, Doctor, I'd like a prescription for some aspirins – my garlic and seaweed pills don't seem to touch my headaches this term, it must be the stress of the O levels and A levels, I suffer *far* more than the girls – and some Elastoplast dressings, they're so much handier than slippery elm for cuts and scalds, and half a dozen pairs of support tights. After all, we pay our taxes, and if we're never ill we must get something for our money. Have you any medical advice you'd particularly like me to follow?'

'Yes. Eat an apple a day.'

'Is that another joke? Perhaps I'd better have the fifth form explain it. Good morning, Doctor,' gathering up her prescriptions. 'I say, you've been jolly D to me, can't I do a favour for you? Come along to our end-of-term concert. Absolutely insist. The fifth form's doing "Hiawatha", though I don't think their heart's in it.'

12 JULY

Terrible row with Sandra this morning. She admits to surgery Mr Attwater, single, thirtyish, works gas showroom, leisure activity apparently reading medical books, well known among Churchford GPs for accurate recital of symptoms of various diseases, serious or trivial, only common factor that he hasn't got them. Also known at General, where inexperienced registrar took his appendix out, dreadful row, though discovered Mr Attwater regularly tries fooling Bart's, Guy's, all top hospitals. This a rare but well-recognized bit of human dottiness.

Mrs Shakespear always throws Mr Attwater out with a flea in ear, indeed wasp. He quite happy to present performance elsewhere (once chewed soap for epileptic fits). When today finally convinced self and Mr Attwater he not suffering from Fallot's tetralogy, explode to Sandra in surgery why let that pest in, can't she see warning on card, underlined in red ink, MÜNCHAUSEN'S SYNDROME? She says thinks that some serious, complex, newly discovered disease. I say you bloody fool, woman, haven't you heard of Baron Münchausen, the legendary liar, God what a bunch of uneducated schoolgirls they let into St Botolph's Nursing School in your day, she says, withdraw that insult immediately or I'll walk out house, I say good, I can get on with my work efficiently, she tells me I vile man, God knows why she married me, particularly as could have had orthopaedic registrar for the asking, spends life doing half my job for me without a damn penny for it, I say not my bloody fault, Inland Revenue's, could knock her off my taxes tomorrow if she my mistress, she says now I'm suggesting she ignoramus harlot? I say that's just the asinine remark I'd expect, she says, Christ, shhhh! the door's open, the patients can hear every word.

Feel awful, but only happened through desperate need of holiday at end of month. Apologize, buy Sandra flowers, Milk Tray, gold-plated ballpoint, thing for putting in cupboards to make smell nice. Begin to wonder about orthopaedic registrar.

24 JULY

Horrified to have letter from my regular locum saying suddenly returning home to Shanka, brother-in-law just appointed minister of health, mad not to enjoy fruits, will probably be president of medical society, or chancellor of university, with a bit of luck both at once. If I do not get holiday shall commit suicide, Sandra doubtless insist on a pact. Wrote to Mrs Charrington regretting that large numbers of gravely ill patients precluded pleasure of seeing 'Hiawatha'.

28 JULY

Amazed to have letter from Mrs Charrington inviting me become doctor to St Ursula's, old Bill Hawesbury (GP other side of golf course) retiring end of this term. Remark re apple obviously missed mark. School genteel despite fifth-form graffiti, duties light, remuneration passable. Say shall consider it after holiday.

31 JULY

Saturday, so morning surgery only – my last until the first Monday of September! Wonderful end-of-term exhilaration, like day abandoned self to drink with Peter Younghusband (MP), both caned for vomiting shandy into school fountain. As dragged luggage from loft heard front door slam, terrified some emergency, relieved to hear son demanding of mother what for lunch as starving.

'Hello, Andy!' I called. 'Come into the bedroom, I'm still packing. You've saved my life, taking over the practice for our hols.'

'No trouble, Dad, as I'm "resting". Do you know, there's almost as much unemployment in the medical as the theatrical profession?' He stood grinning in the doorway. 'Suppose I *never* get another job? How shall humanity enjoy my talents?'

Opened hold-all on the bed. 'Take up politics like Dr Clemenceau of Versailles, Dr Hastings Banda of Malawi or Dr Owen of Limehouse,' I advised. 'Owen's a St Thomas' man, isn't he? Well, boring ward rounds probably inspired his political vision of MPs enjoying strawberry teas on their terrace over the Thames. Pass me that plastic sack.'

'You're not packing this load of drugs? Hardly room for your flip-flops, khaki shorts and pocket chess.'

'I don't trust the habits of foreign doctors. Innuendo is Italian for suppository. Old medical joke.'

'It's a bit alarming, starting general practice from Monday morning,' Andy admitted, 'even though I've been reared in the smell of it, like hay and manure to a farmer's lad. It's like my first day as a houseman, someone had a cardiac arrest, I grabbed the phone and yelled for help, and ten seconds later my own bleep went off. Any advice?'

'Yes. Temper the cold wind of science to the patient shorn of his clothes. To you young chaps in hospital, medicine's as scientific as astronomy, but at this level it gets a bit like astrology. Haven't you invited this other ex-houseman from St Botolph's to share the work? And the house, while we're away. Is he good?'

'Terrific! He's a she.'

'Ah! In my day, the hospital was as masculine as a masons' rugger team,' I reflected. 'We always said that doctors married either nurses, other doctors or barmaids, the only females they ever met. I suppose that's changed?'

'Well, a lot of the nurses now are fellers, though some would make a good wife. The girls who were nurses can now be doctors, and the barmaids have been institutionalized in Bunny Clubs.'

'Toss me that packet of Orange Pekoe. Never travel without it. The tea-bag is as outrageous an affront to civilization as the motorbike. What happened to that bird you brought for the weekend, the vegetarian who talked as if she'd got laryngitis, with a degree in sociology from Runcorn University? Damn condescending female, anyone who calls medicine a branch of the social sciences would hang a Rembrandt in the loo. Anyway, I couldn't understand her jargon. Why say "domestic interface ongoing confrontation" when you mean a flaming family row?'

'She said I lacked empathy, but I think she wanted to move in a higher socio-economic bracket.'

'When *I* was a houseman at St Botolph's I'd started taking life seriously.'

'Did you know, Dad, they still tell the story of you and the theatre sister's knickers?'

AUGUST

1–31 AUGUST

The Algarve. Monchique, 1250 feet up, only two other villas in sight, vast view of Atlantic over Portimao, nearest village five miles down twisting road, sun and indolence, Sandra ten years younger (or possibly self), locals all live to a hundred and fifty and can't be bothered to be ill. Forget I'm a doctor. Lovely.

SEPTEMBER

6 SEPTEMBER

Back to work. Last patient of morning Peter Younghusband (MP), who shared school fountain to be sick in.

'Morning, Richard. Your admirable Mrs Shakespear said charmingly, "The doctor will see you now" – I fancy a phrase loaded with more trouble than any in the language.'

'Why, it's Peter! Oh, I agree, along with, "Pull over to the kerb, sir," and, "There's a young woman outside, but she won't give her name." Have a seat.'

'You're as brown as a nut. Good holiday?'

'Super. Portugal's such a wonderful place, it's a wonder to me Vasco da Gama ever wanted to leave it. And you? Though of course, you chaps don't go back to work until the middle of November.'

'When the talking shop does open for business, it wastes so much time that life is too short for righting the wrongs of the British population, and that of Maidencester East in particular.'

'We haven't met since the Old Boys' dinner. Isn't it amazing how young the masters are getting?'

'Remember, we had a consultation over the port? Thinking about it since, Richard, I've decided to take your advice and have the stomach operation. I feel I can trust the word of a man whose character I know intimately, through sharing a study during its quite disgusting formative years.'

'That's a wise decision, Peter.'

'Though it's going to be torture.'

'Oh come,' I protested. 'We doctors have made surgery these days almost as comfortable as we've made dying.'

'I'm not worried in the slightest about the cutting and carving. But remember I'm a Labour MP, so I'll have to go National Health.'

Groaned sympathetically.

'It's the glaring political disadvantage of the left, quite as bad as Tory members not daring to divorce those dreary wives in big hats.'

Peter Younghusband tall, lean, lined, and strong on ideals. Blue suit, plain white shirt, tie which represented nothing except deplorable taste.

'I don't know why I'm complaining, Richard, it's far worse for our Party leaders. They're ageing gentlemen accustomed to agreeable restaurants, comfortable hotels, amiable companions, intellectual conversation and a whisky-and-soda whenever they feel like it. Once they're under the weather, the poor chaps have to sit for hours on a canvas chair waiting to see a hospital specialist, with nothing but tea, buns and *Woman's Own*.'

'Yes, then undress somewhere as public as the concourse at Euston, to be blanket-bathed by the authorities,' I agreed feelingly. 'Going to hospital's like going to jail – it gets less of a holiday depending on your way of life. At least our ward-sisters compassionately push politicians into side-rooms, on the excuse they're highly infectious, or mentally confused, or of habits likely to disturb the other patients.'

'I'm not complaining about my job, mind you. Would I otherwise have spent a month, decorated with a rosette like a prize bull, being insulted across people's doorsteps to get it? But I fancy that even the *Daily Express* would pity a seedy Labour MP immobilized in some teetotal ward between two bedridden men with the political views of an Alf Garnett and a Clive Jenkins. The only compensation for being ill is that the whole world is nice to you for a change, and brings you grapes. But an MP's health is viewed by the media with the same keen, unsentimental interest as that of the day's runners by the punters. The ghoulish glee of the press! I can't tell you how discouraging it is to read that some passing indisposition is really the galloping staggers, and you'll soon pass beyond recall even by a three-line whip – particularly when things are so tight for the Government that members are going through the lobbies on life-support systems.'

'Is an MP's vote valid when he's suffered brain-death?' I wondered.

'Ah, I see you never listen to Parliament on the radio,' Peter answered.

'Let's have a look at this abdomen.' He exposed the body politic on the couch. 'I say! How did you get this ruddy great bruise up your side?'

'On a demo,' Peter replied mildly. 'What for, now...? I had it last Wednesday, so it was the Environmentalists, Save the Whales and all that...no, they were Monday, and the Right to Work was Saturday, it must have been the Anti-Apartheid lot. I'm a bit old for the protest game, I admit, after all I gave up playing cricket years ago, but even Michael's OK for CND, so long as it isn't raining.'

I palpated his epigastrium. 'I suppose they're only youngsters letting off steam for causes which are irreproachably virtuous?'

'Well, a lot of them would be a bit pushed finding South Africa on the map.'

'Aggression's a part of growing up, of course.'

'You mean, like teething?'

I nodded. 'That hurt?'

'Ouch! I often wonder if every nation suffers an atavistic need for one of those old-fashioned wars – you know, the lads marching off in full gear amid girlish cheers and tumbling rose-petals, with the idea of sticking their highly polished bayonets into some other lad's guts?'

'I think Rollo Basingstoke had better stick his into yours.'

'Beastly Basingstoke! That little squirt? Used to cane him as a prefect, for messy eating. Wouldn't trust him with a knife and fork and a plate of fish and chips, let alone my internal organs.'

'His touch with the cutlery's improved. He's got a knighthood.'

'That only means he's killed several distinguished politicians already.' Peter pulled up his trousers. 'Very well, then. When does he go into action?'

I drew a long, cautious breath. 'Can't say. The private patient pays to avoid waiting. The NHS patient waits to avoid paying. That's the system of medical care we've evolved.' As I washed my hands, I emphasized, 'Half the patients the State pays me to treat today would have been inexpensively dead thirty years ago. God knows about the next thirty, my waiting-room will be like the Tube in the rush-hour.'

'Perhaps I'd better apply for the Chiltern Hundreds? If the hospitals there are to be recommended.'

'I've an idea! Defect to the Social Democrats. Dr Owen wouldn't care how much you paid for your operation.'

'Unfortunately, Dr Owen's operation is all anaesthesia and no surgery.'

'Surely the whole Labour Party isn't staggering through the lobbies hugging hernias and hydroceles, working their way up the national waiting-list?'

'It's infuriating, but a lot of my comrades put themselves down for BUPA, just as smartly as they put their sons down for schools like ours.'

'Might I suggest a statesmanlike compromise? Rollo will get you into a centre of excellence on a high priority basis for a *quid pro quo*. Which means queue-jumping into a decent hospital for a case of port.'

'Out of the question. A socialist would never do that.' Pause. 'Well, hardly ever.'

'I'll write you the usual doctor's letter, you can take it to St Botolph's via Berry Brothers. I noticed at OBs' dinner Rollo was into the Graham's 63.'

8 SEPTEMBER

Five patients asked today, Where was the young doctor? Seemed crestfallen to learn he a passing phenomenon. Proud, but slightly nettled. Assume patients benefited from instant availability of second opinion by another St Botolph's doctor. As only one spare bedroom used, a twenty-four service.

15 SEPTEMBER

Battle of Britain Day. Can it *possibly* be forty-odd years since youthful eyes watched history being written in vapour-trails? Appropriate first patient.

'I'm worried about the war, Doctor.'

'Then avoid it. Keep well clear of Londonderry and Lebanon, the Euphrates and all Middle Eastern embassies. Odd, isn't it, Mr Handcross, how wars since Hitler have gone local? Nobody can afford the big international projects any more.'

'I mean World War III.' Mr Handcross small, bald, sweaty, suffers anxiety neurosis. 'A man called from Brentford trying to sell me a nuclear shelter, and I wondered if it was a worthwhile investment.'

'Splendid idea!' The things people ask doctors. 'Stock it with tinned food – avoid baked beans, in the confined space,' I advised. 'And something for morale. I'd recommend a few cases of the Dom Perignon '71. Even if there isn't a nuclear war it'll be kept in excellent condition, quite as good as the ice houses dug in Victorian gardens. Good morning.'

'But what will happen, Doctor, when the mushroom cloud goes up over Sevenoaks?' Mr Handcross persevered.

'I'll tell you exactly.' Always best if patients know what to expect. 'First, quite a wind, 800 m.p.h., flattens everything for ten miles. Then some old-fashioned thermal radiation, just like fire bombs in the London blitz, except it sets absolutely everything ablaze for twenty miles in all directions. Did you know, in Hiroshima they first thought that the Americans had dropped a perfectly ordinary bomb and hit the gasworks, with the flames spreading along the gas-pipes into everybody's kitchen? Japanese surgeon told me. Interesting.'

I rubbed my hands. 'Next come the gamma rays. And of course fall-out. Scientists in Washington have calculated precisely the dose of radiation needed to kill Americans, which is half – I think this is interesting, too – the dose which scientists in London have estimated as necessary to kill *us*. Jolly complimentary to the hardy Island Race, don't you think? Either that, or the Home Office made a cock-up of its arithmetic.'

'Not much anyone can do about a holocaust, I suppose?'

'On the contrary,' I corrected him cheerfully, 'it is entirely under control by the Department of Health and Social Security. Their Circular HDC(77)1 disposes of nuclear wars. A week before the attack – '

'How shall we know, Doctor?'

'Our chaps at Fylingdale will tell us. Every patient languishing in our hospitals and institutions will be sent home. There's an advantage of nuclear weapons to start with, a lot of them wouldn't otherwise be reunited with their families for years. I believe the Fylingdale warning is

116

only four minutes, but perhaps they'll be able to manage a little longer on the day.'

'I suppose that'll be the end of the National Health as we know it,' he suggested miserably.

'Not a bit. Apply and adapt, rather than innovate – a splendid principle that's served this country since the Norman Conquest. On receipt of the warning, the NHS will disperse its equipment over as wide an area as possible, an exercise thoroughly tested by all the nicking that goes on from hospitals. The staff will disperse, too. The medical profession is too valuable to be turned into a load of crispy noodles. Each health area will be administered by a dictator, just like now. As all the country's hospitals will have collapsed – you must have noticed, many look ripe for rubble with the passing of an overloaded lorry – all casualties will go to local authority rest centres.'

'They sound quite cosy,' Mr Handcross observed more hopefully.

'I expect they'll be perfectly tolerable, with the Women's Royal Voluntary Service handing out tea and ham sandwiches. The rest centres will be run by local GPs and dentists. A doctor in Chippenham wants the medical staff issued with shotguns, to discourage people from looting the penicillin. All should go very smoothly, so long as there isn't an ambulancemen's strike. Good morning.'

'Could *I* do anything, Doctor? If I wasn't in my shelter, that is.'

'Lots. The circular says, "Casualties would have to provide as much basic nursing care for each other as their injuries allowed." It'll be the only DIY war in history. Good morning.'

'What's the odds? Perhaps you're right, they'll never drop it.'

'Oh, you can die of nuclear radiation peacefully in your own home,' I informed him helpfully. 'The National Radiological Protection Board says that five hundred people a year are killed by a radioactive miasma from their own bricks and mortar. Paying the mortgage on them, too. It's to do with the decaying uranium in stone, particularly granite. Must be a lot of it about in Scotland. The cure is for everyone always to keep their windows open, which would wreck the government's energy policy. Good morning.'

'I'll buy the shelter, Doctor. As soon as it's installed under the lawn, I'll go inside, lock the door and stay there.'

'I should. Living can seriously damage your health. *Good morning!*'

27 SEPTEMBER

Dreadfully busy surgery. Those women made pregnant by last Christmas appear with their babies, all in need of certificates, innoculations, assurances that infant has only one heart, normal intelligence or just his father's lovely eyes. Also, new batch just made pregnant by package holidays. Congratulate self have maintained diary for nine months, though probably more value to future scholars if practice of medicine in Churchford not continually complicated by family, friends and Fate (Mrs Blessington).

28 SEPTEMBER

'Might I bring my egg, peas and chips to your table? I'm a GP, just visiting a patient here in the General, my old friend the major, actually. Thought I'd lunch in the staff canteen after reading in *The Times* how some talkative chap who runs one of the unions – probably yours, but of course no offence – wants the gap between hospital doctors and hospital porters drastically reduced, financially, socially and culturally. I'd like you to know – I see from your lapel you're a porter– that I absolutely agree.'

No comment. Big, blond, lardaceous young chap in brown overall, goes on eating sausage, beans and chips. Probably after hard morning hauling trolleys loaded with sterile supplies, laundry, garbage, corpses, etc. along hospital corridors you are left with good appetite.

Churchford General Hospital sprawling institution on North Downs off London Road. Partly red-brick former workhouse, partly long concrete buildings raised for Royal Air Force (era of Spitfire), partly odd blocks apparently erected when government happened to have the money, and spanking new tower opened by royalty but closed for first six months over inter-union difference as who screw in light bulbs, etc. In fact, typical NHS centre of healing. Could have lunched in doctors' mess, but case of port

(Graham's '63) from Peter Younghusband (MP) jogged conscience that I becoming crusty Tory (as most GPs). Must mix socially, exchange views of life, politics, etc. with the masses, who usually I tell simply get on couch and take clothes off.

'We've a lot to learn from each other, you and me,' I conceded, picking up knife and fork. Canteen yellow-walled, yellow table-tops, yellow lighting, makes all eaters look suffering jaundice, all food deep-fried (mostly is). 'Disraeli's tradition of One Nation, you know, which the Tories always discover when they're in trouble. Though I don't suppose you see *The Times*,' it occurred to me. 'Bums and tits and horoscopes more in your line, eh? But you'd find a lot of interest in it, who's dead for instance, and we doctors could pick up a lot from you about permutations and pop stars, would you kindly pass the HP sauce?'

'Whazzat?'

'I'll make a long arm. A jolly good meal you chaps can get, if it's cold it's dirt cheap. I expect you're keen to learn the different view taken of medicine by doctors and porters? You've heard of Henry VIII?'

He mouthed fork loaded with orange beans.

'Everybody's heard of Henry VIII, I'm sure, even in comprehensives where they seem to teach only picketing and soccer hooliganism.' I smiled. 'I make that remark in the Pickwickian sense, you understand.'

Went on forking beans.

'It all goes back to Henry VIII's dissolution of the monastries. Before that, you see, the country ran a surplus of monks and nuns, who not only tended the sick enthusiastically but *for free*. Now, I'm not suggesting you NUPE lot should take a page out of their missal. Indeed, if you regard the *raison d'être* – that means "the purpose of existence" – of the National Health Service as providing you with the same job on ever-increasing wages for life, so do the employees of all nationalized industries. And jolly good luck to them, I say, even if we could still be the world's major suppliers of horseshoes, crinoline hoops and puffing billies. You look a pretty intelligent young fellow, I'm sure you follow my argument. Are you happy in your work?'

'Whazzat?'

'Mind you, I've nothing against trade unions,' I told him disarmingly, 'unlike the major, who politically is not so much to the right of, but out of sight of, Genghis Khan. Yes, my friend the major describes trade unions as dimwits run by smart Alecs, and I'd like to tell you that I don't agree, in fact I'd say myself, from the oratory at the Trades Union Congress, quite the opposite. How's your lunch?'

Pronged and champed spiky sheaf of chips, so assumed satisfactory.

'The major's in for a prostate, that's a senior citizen's tonsillectomy,' I explained. 'All well, I'm glad to say, the head plumber here is outstanding. I don't know whether you've reflected, my dear chap, how we doctors become of importance when we *start* work, you porters only when you stop. I'm sure with the fair-mindedness of the British worker you'll appreciate any surgeon's viewpoint, when he's told who he can or can't operate on by some bugger without an O level, probably just jumped out of a banana plantation, though luckily the medical profession suffers none of the prejudices of ordinary people, may I have the vinegar?'

'Whazzat?'

'I can reach it, these chips need a bit of soaking, they're rather like deep-fried South African biltong, which I expect you know is strips of sun-dried buffalo. Might I ask your views on private practice?'

Waited politely while he masticated cheese and lettuce roll on the side, but apparently not framed thoughts.

'I expect you'd prefer to see paying medicine outlawed, like this odd trades union fellow I mentioned. Nothing wrong with that opinion, nothing at all, except it's lunatic, the National Health would rapidly suffocate under the weight of the national illness without the life-support system of private medicine. Though I thoroughly agree with this exhibitionistic paranoic jumped-up trade union squit, you and I *both* need an efficient NHS. If it employs at the moment twice the porters it wants, and half the doctors it needs, if your job has been convincingly demonstrated to be performed in quarter of the time by volunteers during a strike, well, that's only bad man-management, isn't it? Though I must warn you porter-chappies –'

Shook finger over sauce bottle. He gazed blankly.

'You'll soon be as redundant as steelworkers, my dear sir, the DIY hospital has arrived. Yes, already! Could you pass the salt, I'm not sure about this egg, I think they've fried the Brillo pad.'

'Whazzat?'

'It's less of a hospital than a day clinic, of course,' I explained reaching for the cruet. 'A branch of the Wellington private hospital, which has such an excellent bedside wine list. It's run by American capitalists – dreadfully sorry – ninety-nine quid a day, including use of operating theatre and light refreshments, very reasonable, I'm sure you'll agree, though naturally the hackwork comes extra. You turn up with your varicose veins or hernia after breakfast, you go home without them after tea, the wife and kids rally round and nurse you. What's wrong with that? Vets do it to the family pet every day. Mark my words, it's a trend, NHS hospitals will soon be as empty of manual labour as a Japanese car factory. Push your own trolley to the operating theatre, well it's not half as discouraging as digging your own grave. I suppose these peas aren't polystyrene beads from the out-patients' upholstery?'

'Whazzat?'

'I do hope you don't think I'm class conscious?' I remarked defensively. 'I always say, we doctors know only two classes, alive and dead. Indeed, to quote Dr Jonathan Miller – maybe you saw *The Body in Question* on the box – medicine is a philistine profession, attracting its recruits with the assurance of a respect and importance in society. Nothing anti-social in that motivation, I'm sure you'll agree, it's how democracy works. Might I ask, what would *you* mean by the word "democracy"?'

He was into the baked jam roll with bright yellow custard.

'Might I tell you what I – or Milton in *Paradise Regained* – mean by "democracy"?' I enquired politely. 'Quite simple, we mean government by the people. Now, you'd use it for government by a few rather nasty people, whose one delight is seeing that the rest of us are all kept equally miserable. Same principle with "adult", which now seems to mean infantile, or "gay" which can mean positively suicidal. Or "sensible", which means what trade union leaders think, or "divisive politics", which means not complying with their wishes PDQ. But I'm beginning to sound like the major. Have you handled him?'

'Whazzat?'

'I fear he has not been his old self since he suffered the male menopause on the Thursday afternoon before Christmas.' A chip ricocheted from the yellow plastic flooring. 'Do you know, he was far more worried about his operation than once he was about hitting the Hun for six under Monty. I reminded him how Mr Macmillan became even more unflappable after a prostatectomy in 1963, even General de Gaulle had one, though he funked the operation for years, instead they inserted a little tube, I wonder if it had a cork with *mis en bouteilles dans nos caves*?'

'Whazzat?'

He gulped his Tizer. I invited, 'Might I ask your name, sir?'

'Dubrovnik.'

'That's a – if I may say – slightly unusual name.'

'Dubrovnik,' he repeated. 'Dubrovnik. Dubrovnik. Dubrovnik.'

'Ah! You are some sort of foreigner?'

'Dubrovnik.' He stared as though I were an idiot. 'Jus' come Dubrovnik. No spik English.'

He stood and left. 'Oh, well,' I reflected, 'perhaps it was for the best. I think I'll give my sieved apple-and-raspberry jelly a miss.'

30 SEPTEMBER

Memorable day. At last the Vowson file is closed!

For almost ten years, the case has held for me the same fascination and frustration as some unsolved crime of great enormity on the files of Scotland Yard. I reproduce the papers *in toto*.

> *The Surgery*
> *Foxglove Lane*
> *Churchford*
> *8 January 1974*

Dear Sir,

My patient Mrs Emily Vowson was discharged from the General Hospital last Thursday after an operation for bunions. Unfortunately, she was postoperatively handed by the nurse the wrong set of dentures. Her horror at discovering yesterday that she had been eating with another's teeth is matched by her indignation that someone else is munching with hers. I should appreciate your restituting these oral changelings as a matter of urgency.

RICHARD GORDON, MB BCHIR

Churchford General Hospital
28 February 1974

Dear Dr Gordon,

In reply to yours of 8th ult, you will be aware that the hospital acts as gratuitous bailee of patients' property, and can therefore accept liability only on production of a receipt for the teeth, witnessed by a third party. The situation is covered by Department of Health and Social Security Circular HMC(49) 107. Re the teeth now in situ, these would appear to fall under section 48 of the National Assistance Act 1948, which protects a patient's property outside the hospital. Thus no action can be taken, unless your patient is of unsound mind, and can apply to the Court of Protection under the Mental Health Act 1959.

H R T PROUDFOOT
Administrator

Shire Hall
Maidencester
29 March 1974

Dear Dr Gordon,

I regret that I cannot reply to your letter of 1 March about Mrs Vowson's teeth, addressed to me at Regional Hospital Board level. Under Sir Keith Joseph's reorganization of the National Health Service to last from 1 April for the rest of the century, I am now Area Health Authority, to which all correspondence must be addressed.

MYRTLE SOURTHORPE
Secretary

Churchford General Hospital
6 January 1975

Dear Dr Gordon,

Mr Proudfoot having emigrated to Riyadh, I am somewhat confused by your letter of 30 May 1974. As Mrs Vowson entered hospital for her bunions but lost her teeth, she would appear to have a valid complaint for wrongful operation. This should be forwarded to the Health Service Commissioner (the "Ombudsman" in popular parlance) established by the NHS Reorganization Act 1973.

ARTHUR HOBBITT
Acting Administrator

Churchford General Hospital
9 December 1976

Dear Dr Gordon,

I am replying to your letter of last February on behalf of Mr Hobbitt, who after the most unfortunate incident widely reported in the press will be away for some years. I note that the painful teeth which Mrs Vowson reports are not, in fact, hers. I would remind you that complaints against the hospital can be made only by the person concerned, as clearly directed by HM(66) 15, amplified in RHB(51)80.

GERTRUDE NULLS
Assistant Administrator

Alexander Fleming House
Elephant and Castle
SE1
15 June 1977

Sir,

The Secretary of State acknowledges your telegram of 6 January, but regrets that public funds are unavailable to help Mrs Vowson with a nationwide campaign for the examination of all mature women's false teeth, comparable with that for cervical smears.

A O WINKLER
Deputy Secretary

BBC TV Centre
Wood Lane
W12 7RJ
29 July 1977

Dear Sir,

The Director-General is in receipt of your letter dated 16 June, but regrets that he does not consider Mrs Vowson's teeth a suitable subject for the *Panorama* programme.

EGBERT FLEURY
Assistant to the Assistant Controller

Thames Television
306 Euston Road
NW1
25 August 1977

Dear Richard,

Thanks ever so much for your lovely long letter of 1 August, but Eamonn just can't fit in a programme called *These Are Your Teeth*. You can't win them all, can you! Carry on viewing!

Hi!

POLLY
Personal Assistant

New Scotland Yard
Broadway
SW1
September 1977

Dear Sir,

The Commissioner has your communication dated 30th ult but wishes to state that the Missing Persons Department traces only missing persons whole, not portions thereof.

J BLINKS
Chief Inspector

3 October 1977

THE EDITOR REGRETS THAT YOUR PAPER *A Case of Total Dental Transplantation (False)* IS UNSUITABLE FOR PUBLICATION IN THE *BRITISH MEDICAL JOURNAL.*

From the Sun, *18 October 1977*

WHO'S GOT GRANNIE'S GNASHERS?

Emily Vowson (61) went into Churchford Hospital, Kent, for her feet…and came out with someone else's teeth!

'Of course I don't like using another person's dentures,' said Emily in the £15,000 bungalow she shares with husband Arthur (63) and cat Jollyboy. 'Would you? But I've got to eat, haven't I, and we must learn to put up with a lot of things in life we don't like.'

THAT'S IT, GRAN! IF WE ALL PUT UP WITH OUR LOT INSTEAD OF *MOANING*, THIS COUNTRY WOULD STICK OUT ITS CHEST AGAIN! JUST LIKE OUR PIC OF MOIRA (16$^1/_2$), A TRAINEE DENTAL ASSISTANT WHO WANTS TO BE A TRAINEE DENTIST!

10 Downing Street
SW1
18 May 1979

Dear Dr Gordon,

Mrs Thatcher thanks you for the congratulations in your letter of 5 May. The Prime Minister is, of course, deeply interested in teeth, as in all social questions.

ALISTAIR PINN
Press Officer

Buckingham Palace
20 May 1979

Dear Sir,

I am commanded by Her Majesty The Queen to thank you for your letter dated yesterday. Her Majesty has this morning dispatched it to the Department of Health and Social Security.

ILKLEY
Comptroller Gold Wand

From The Times, *29 June 1979*

The minister replied that an outbreak of foot and mouth disease in the Churchford area was ill-founded press speculation. (Cheers, cries of 'Shame,' 'Resign,' 'Bring back Ted.')

Elm Park Mansions
Park Walk
London,
SW10
28 November 1980

Dear Dr Gordon,

Sorry I can't use your lovely teeth stuff. Nature is creeping up on art. Nothing wrong with that! Here's a pound.

HENRY ROOT

Maidencester
11 September 1981

Dear Dr Gordon,

I regret that I cannot take up the matter of Mrs Vowson's teeth, as the Area Health Authority is shortly to disappear under Mr Patrick Jenkin's reorganization of the NHS for the rest of the century.

MYRTLE SIM (*Mrs*)
Secretary

Radio 2, 23 December 1981

JIMMY WIGGAN:...well, there, *that's* put you in the seasonal mood, and our next request comes from Mrs Emily Vowson in Kent...hope you're surviving the bitter snow down there among the hop poles...no, it's from Mrs Vowson's *doctor*! Who says the National Health isn't a real, *caring* service? The man with the little black bag wants played for his patient – and we all hope you'll be fit and well again soon, Emily, we *sincerely* do – is a golden oldie, came out way, waaaay back, 'All I Want For Christmas Is My Two Front Teeth'. That's not asking for much!

Alexander Fleming House
Elephant and Castle
SE1
24 September 1982

Dear Dr Gordon,

Your letter of 8 January has just been passed to me. I am delighted to say that misplaced dentures from hospitals all over the country have accumulated in my office, and now completely fill a tea-chest, which I am forwarding by BR for you to make your selection. I do not wish the tea-chest back, not in any circumstances. Keep it in case the occasion arises again. Kind regards.

SALLY GOODBODY
Assistant Secretary

Churchford General Hospital
24 September 1982

Dear Dr Gordon,

The collapse through dry-rot of Ward 10 produced in the rubble the enclosed dentures, which Mrs Agworth, our head cleaner, said you lost some years ago.

EDGAR RUMROD
Administrator (Works)

Churchford General Hospital
27 September 1982

Dear Dr Gordon,

I note from your letter returning the teeth that Mrs Vowson has now departed to Abraham's Bosom. If you will send me her full address (including postal code), I shall be happy to forward them at NHS expense.

K J TICKLER
Senior Administrator

Alexander Fleming House
Elephant and Castle
SE1
29 September 1982

Sir,

The Secretary of State is not amused.

Q R L CROCKER-BRIGHT
Under Secretary

OCTOBER

1 OCTOBER

Michaelmastide, the world back to work – professors and students, judges and criminals, doctors and patients. People not ill during summer as have garden, holidays, picnics, seaside, Wimbledon etc. to keep their minds off it.

'Hello, darling. Heavy evening surgery?'

'Ghastly. Everyone's got muscular dystrophy.'

Cool evening. Fire. Twilight. Sandra on living-room sofa, reading Delia Smith.

Surprised. 'Really? But that's terribly rare, isn't it?'

'There was a programme about it last night on TV. Couple of weeks ago, there was a big feature about lice, and the patients turned up with everything from typhus fever to pediculosis pubis.'

'What pubis?'

'Crabs.' Leant down to tickle Galen on hearthrug. 'You'd be surprised, even the most respectable middle-aged ladies. Well, nice to know they've still got the itch, as it were.' Throw self in chair, pick up *Radio Times*. 'Oh, God! tonight the BBC are doing schizophrenia, which means everyone will appear tomorrow morning with split personalities, both demanding prescriptions. Where's the gin?'

Sandra passed bottle, she already at it. 'Just relax, dear, and think about something nice.'

'Right-ho.' Pour therapeutic dose gin and ton. 'Where shall we go this year for our autumn conference?'

'Oh, here's the updated list from BMA House.' Passed thick sheaf across hearth. 'Arrived this morning.'

'Let's have a look…how about Czechoslovakia this time? I see there's a Symposium on Human Milk at a place called Hradec Kralove, or perhaps that's the name of the chap in charge. Or Hungary?' I suggested vaguely. 'Veröcemaros seems an interesting spot, Congress on Immunological Methodology.'

Frowned. 'What's that?'

'Search me. But does it matter?'

'After the dreadful weather since we got home from Portugal I *must* see some sun.'

'International Symposium on Fertility Control any appeal to you? That's in Tunis. Or Emergency and Disaster Medicine in New Delhi?'

'Not *that* much sun, Richard,' she objected. 'You know how I go like a boiled beetroot,'

'Symposium on Electrolyte and Water Transport Across Gastrointestinal Epithelia? That sounds fascinating. Oh, it's in Manchester. Out of the question. Fifth World Congress on Sexology? Held in Jerusalem. Enough to make Our Lord turn in His grave, if only He'd stayed there.'

'Perhaps we should play safe and go to Spain again?'

'There's some Odonto-Stomatology at Valencia,' I noticed. 'Which makes a change from the Pathology of Ulcers in Fuengerola last year. But what's the rush?' Drained gin and ton. 'There's over two hundred international meetings between now and Christmas, on this list alone. That's not mentioning the ones convened in nice sunny places by drug companies to discuss this year's batch of breakthroughs. The doctor's thirst for knowledge is unquenchable, a sort of intellectual diabetes. I'll have another gin.'

'Of course, it's nice for doctors to enjoy a break,' Sandra said tenderly. 'And for me it's a change, at least, to see another lot of doctors' wives. But I sometimes *do* wonder a weeny bit if any of these meetings do the slightest good.'

'Tremendous good!' Settled back with refill. 'Don't you realize, it's one of the few global growth industries? The livelihood of whole towns, of some entire small countries, depends exclusively upon conferences.'

'Yes, but does it do any good to the *doctors*?'

'To their morale. Everyone seems more important when they're somewhere else. Even the Pope. Some doctors orbit the earth so constantly, I doubt if they've see a patient for years. They're the stars of the lecture circuit, the Pam Ayres of the medical profession.'

'Perhaps *you* should try lecturing, dear?' Sandra suggested brightly. 'After all, you were wonderful at the golf club dinner.'

'The story about the doctor's budgie went down pretty well,' I agreed modestly. 'I suppose it's easy enough, once you get in the swing. When Freud travelled to America, or Pasteur only from Lille to Paris, they had something to say. Now any old waffle will get you to Rio or Rotorua or Reykjavik, so long as you've sufficient boxes of coloured slides. What's that slim folder?'

She tossed it across the rug. 'It's all about the BMA Congress this month.'

'In San Diego!' I opened it with wonder. 'The old Beem really is doing itself well, I thought the only organizations who held conferences in flashy places like that were *Playboy* and Jehovah's Witnesses. Forty glossy pages…'

'What are the BMA going to discuss in San Diego, dear?'

'Doesn't say. Just Clinical Sessions, Medical Visits, Visit to US Navy Medical Base and Farewell Banquet. What lovely photos, silver sands and blue seas! Medicine can be great fun for the doctors, if not always for the patients.'

'But San Diego!' Sandra exclaimed, concerned. 'Miles and miles away on the lush coasts of California. How much will it sting everyone?'

'Oh, it'll cost a packet for each doctor – and "accompanying person", as the BMA puts it with expected medical tact. Not that it matters. The whole of page 35 is advice from a tax expert, describing how you can fiddle the lot so long as you doze through at least one lecture.'

Sandra sighed. 'Sometimes, my sweet, I wish we could simply enjoy an ordinary second holiday, like so many other people.'

'So do I, but on a six per cent pay rise we can't possibly afford it.'

2 OCTOBER

Decide on New York and Whither Gastroduodenostomy? Never been to the Big Apple, only San Francisco, the World's Sweetheart.

3 OCTOBER

Sunday, Jilly home. Starts tomorrow as student in the wards of St Botolph's, as last summer passed 2nd MB in anatomy and physiology. Now owns stethoscope, dreadfully proud of. This practical appliance has same symbolism as cleric's collar, lawyer's wig, or chef's tall white hat. Jilly scared of handling live people (cf. anatomy). Reassure her, the medical system will carry her along, as the military system carries Sandhurst cadets. After a couple of months in the wards, the medical student develops a sense of human relations which escapes many – businessmen, politicians, academics, administrators – all their lives. Mind, the people all in dead trouble, which helps.

18 OCTOBER

'This is your captain speaking. If there's a doctor on the aircraft, will he make himself known to the cabin crew. Thank you.'

Look round nervously. Lights dimmed. Full plane. Sandra asleep beside me. In fact, all asleep, even maniacal children been charging up and down aisle since leaving Heathrow. Inspect watch. 2 a.m. In London or in New York? Completely forget if changed it before take-off. Toss aside blanket, make way jacketless to small recess emitting light and clinking noises.

'Er…hostess…stewardess…?'

Pretty, dark-haired, mid-twenties, snappy uniform, make-up as flawless as colouring of rose petals. 'Can I get you anything to drink, sir?'

'I'm sorry intruding into your kitchenette, but I'm a doctor.'

'Oh, yes, sir.' Secured metal door on stack of dirty plastic food trays. 'An elderly lady at the back felt poorly after that little bout of turbulence, but she's better now.'

'*Little bout of turbulence?* I was scared stiff,' I confess readily. 'All that shaking and shuddering, those bouts of weightlessness, that shower of plastic cutlery… I honestly thought we were going to find ourselves ten miles up in an instant airliner construction kit. Surely we're not far from the Bermuda Triangle?' I recall with horror. 'Where aeroplanes disappear as mysteriously as cancelled British Rail trains? How I admired you, continuing to preside over dinner with the steely insouciance of Lady Macbeth when her husband keeps seeing Banquo.'

'Are you sure I can't get you anything to drink, sir?'

'Absolutely! I read all through the traveller's medical guide before leaving home. We doctors take sensible precautions over our health, even if our patients think us fusspot spoilsports. This cabin air simply dehydrates all the passengers, like rows of finnan haddies hanging in the smoker at Aberdeen. And alcohol,' I continued severely, 'only accentuates the process by inhibiting the pituitary antidiuretic hormone. Didn't you know?'

'We pick up items of information of all sorts from the passengers, sir.'

'Particularly *fizzy* drinks!' I emphasize. She stands politely in her vibrating metal grotto, as poised as a picture in *Vogue*. 'In the rarefied atmosphere – I'm sure you realize that you and I are really chatting in the Simplon Pass, flying at sea-level pressure would mean constructing the plane like an army tank – those sort of drinks blow up your stomach worse than heavy meals. So why do airlines propel passengers steaks like rafts on rivers of champagne?' I asked.

'The passengers find it helps to pass the time, sir.'

'Like the inhabitants of the Hebrides.'

'We don't fly there, sir.'

'I mean, you've read Boswell? He said they wished for meals from the cravings of vacuity of mind, as well as from the desire of eating.'

'I have little time for anything except sleep between flights, sir.'

'You must have come from a modelling school.'

'I come from Godalming, sir.'

'Do you know what you represent?'

'I am a member of the cabin crew's union, sir, we are obliged to be.'

'You are a masterstroke of psychology. Even the most macho male can be terrified of flying, but the airlines have discovered, along with Gilbert and Sullivan, that "When a man's afraid, a beautiful maid is a cheering sight to see." '

'Most of our male passengers are elderly, sir.'

'What of it? My old friend the Major has an eye for a pretty girl like Ian Botham for a long hop, and admits to having put his sexual organs on a care and maintenance basis. *I* get dreadfully agitated travelling anywhere anyhow, I'm one of the few people to develop jet lag on the Bakerloo line. You're familiar with Freud's term *Reisenangst?*'

'The other stewardess on this section is fluent in German, sir, I speak only Tamil.'

'Perhaps you were told in training, Freud interpreted dreams of flying as dreams of sexual excitement?'

'I don't believe it was mentioned, sir.'

'In those days of Baron von Richthofen flying was daring, now it's no longer an adventure but a mass activity, even somewhat boring. The same with sex. What do you think?'

'We are instructed not to become familiar with the passengers, sir.'

'Of course, the current fashion for psychiatry is entirely due to the airlines,' I inform her. 'By causing the collapse of the shipping industry. All our quarrelsome, hypochondriacal, egotistical and sex-ridden patients, we now get rid of by sending to a psychiatrist. In the old days, we sent them on a world cruise. I was once a ship's doctor, you know, with brass buttons and gold braid, even hair and a waistline, if you can imagine it.'

'We advise overweight passengers to remove their shoes during the flight, sir. Would you care for me to freshen up your head?'

Reflect stewardesses achieve sharp sense of human relations as quickly as medical students. Job probably endurable only by treating all passengers as harmless nutters.

A phone buzzes. 'Excuse me, sir –' Takes a brief message. 'Could you see the old lady? She's poorly again.'

'We doctors are always on call, even to sort out turbulent old ladies.'

'To the left out of the galley, sir.'

Follow her towards the tail. Small grey-haired figure leaning across seat.

'Good God! She isn't poorly. She's dead.'

'Thank you, sir.'

'But…but isn't it an appalling calamity on a crowded aircraft?' I exclaim.

'Not at all, sir. It occurs quite frequently, with people returning to their homeland to die and not quite making it. We wrap them in a blanket and wedge them in the toilet with pillows. It takes only a few minutes.'

'If Macbeth had married an air stewardess, he'd never have ended up in all that trouble,' I tell her admiringly. 'And then you can get me something to drink.'

29 OCTOBER

Home. Exhausted by conference. Gastroduodenostomy is high-class piece of stomach surgery for peptic ulcers, many pros and cons, decided lectures likely to be rarefied, but anyway no time because of Fifth Avenue, Statue of Liberty, Lincoln Center, Rockefeller Center, also the Met, Moma, Frick and Gug (art galleries, American millionaires having looted European collections like benevolent Goerings), plus Broadway and 42nd Street (very porno, indeed gynaecological).

Inaugural conference cocktail party terrific, top of World Trade Center downtown, view across Manhattan at dusk, lights like global takeover by glow-worms. We met plastic surgeon just arrived from Los Angeles, three-cornered moustache, lean, tanned, eager, restive, in fact jumpy. Enquire why he attending conference on surgery deep within abdomen? He says, excuse to patients for escaping latest wife, who threatening him with arrest for assault, larceny, rape, defamation, moral turpitude, etc. (Californian married life hectic).

He says, I from Olde England? Do I know Goat and Compasses? He did six months' exchange job at St Botolph's. Instant lifelong friends. He says, incredible, respect paid to English doctors by patients. I say, relic of squire-tenant relationship, which after all did everybody a bit of good, maybe touch forelock but squire provide new roof, Christmas goodies, protection against hard world. He says, all US patients crazy about suing doctors, swears the bitches arrive for consultation with blank court orders in handbags, will soon examine them along with attorney in white jacket. Goddam case going on now in LA with this navel, maybe he left it half-an-inch out of true after fat-whittling operation, but patient a professional belly-dancer, screaming is artist, career wrecked as if some guy amputated Michelangelo's right hand or castrated Casanova.

After several martinis, confesses miserably he ruined by success like some unstable movie star, was happy out-of-town surgeon, comfortable ranch-type home, loving wife who baked cakes, shopped at A & P, thought Julie Andrews wonderful. Hit big time in plastics, discovered all Californians were gold-plated, changed lifestyle, house in Santa Monica, Ferrari and Mercedes, huge pool (underwater illumination), parties, new young wife, though proved very excitable, changed her twice, present one like Bo Derek but definitely psychopathic, needs earn more than two Harley Street consultants just to pay standing charges on past wives. Wishes gone to Nebraska and operated on pig-farmers instead, insisted taking us to supper at Sardi's (theatrical), as likes observing beautiful actresses with the eye of Fabergé examining gold *objets d'art*, or maybe hard-hat man contemplating New York construction sites.

In Sardi's, after more martinis, thanks Jesus for new tit-filleting operation, will pay off those tramps he married. I say, why fillet tit? He says, leaves the nipple. I say, for what purpose, then? He says, hell, men like it and a woman must have something to show through her shirt. I say, you fillet tit for disease? He says, no, as a preventative measure. I say, you mean, like cutting off a chap's legs in case he falls down and breaks an ankle? He says, that's more or less the idea, but the surgeons have got to live as well as the patients. Starts to cry, gets a cab, commands pick up unopened bag at Hilton drive on to Kennedy, going back to LA, Bo Derek wife probably paranoid schizophrenic but he loves her. Feel there's a moral in all this.

31 OCTOBER

Read in the Sunday papers of Sir Rollo Basingstoke 'the Harley Street specialist' treating the Queen. Rollo becoming terribly grand. Recall when we shared lodgings, he took intense dislike to landlady, used to masturbate in the bath in hope of making her mysteriously pregnant.

NOVEMBER

1 NOVEMBER

Pull back bedroom curtains, exclaim to Sandra country under several feet of snow. She says from bed I exaggerate as usual, only an inch or two, I say what the hell? Dusting of snowflakes British Rail grinds to a halt, airports closed, roads vast traffic jam, entire workforce walks out as factories too chilly. Meanwhile, we doctors must perform errands of mercy. Luckily, few patients at morning surgery (inclement weather improves nation's health dramatically), so could begin errands early.

Start car, it makes noise like load of old iron joining scrapyard, steam emerges, curse vilely, move in jerks along icy road to Straker's Garage. Dozen cars inside workshop, young men in blue overalls whistling and banging them about with spanners. Mr Straker, tall, sandy, steel-rimmed glasses, grave, fiftyish, in clean white coat.

'Good morning, Doctor! And a pretty sharp one, too. What can I do for you?'

'I feel a bit of a fool, Mr Straker.' Always anxious when necessary to see Mr Straker, though utmost confidence placing self in his hands, particularly with a name standing so high in his profession. 'I expect I'm just wasting your time, when everyone knows how terribly busy you always are —'

'Now, Doctor —' Kind but firm. 'No customer can ever waste my time. If you've taken the trouble to come and see me, there must be something wrong, mustn't there?'

'As a matter of fact, I'm afraid there is,' I agreed unhappily.

'When did it all start?'

'Let me think, now. Last Whitsun, when I drove to my Aunt Annie, who lives in Dymchurch, and who's pushing eighty, but would you believe it doesn't need glasses to read the paper, not the headlines that is –'

'Tell me what the trouble is *now*, Doctor,' Mr Straker cut in.

'It's this throbbing sensation, deep down.'

'H'm. Only the throbbing sensation?'

'Yes. No, I mean. There's a low whirring noise.'

'Ah! A throbbing sensation *and* a low whirring noise. H'm, h'm.'

'Nothing…nothing serious, I hope?' I enquired pathetically.

'I trust not, I trust not…but…of course, we shall have to see.'

'I mean, it's not likely to be a major job? Not having to…go in?'

Mr Straker thoughtfully tapped ballpoint against teeth.

'I've been frightened of that, ever since I first noticed something the matter,' I confessed, 'but I rather foolishly hoped it was all imagination.'

He ordered, 'Just open your bonnet, will you? Wider, please. H'm, h'm, h'm. When did you last have a regular check up?'

I answered, flurried, 'I know I *should*, but I never seem to find the time.'

'Dear me! Well, we do advise it, particularly in this age-bracket. Prevention is better than cure, you know.' Clearly, only feelings of humanity prevented his scolding me. Felt foolish, guilty, unworthy, servile. 'Is *that* where you have the throbbing?' he asked.

'Yes!' Amazed at such cleverness. 'Precisely there.'

'I think I'd like a specimen of your water. We really should see if it contains any oil.'

Gripped by a chill colder than the weather. Did Mr Straker not credit me with the intelligence, gleaned from all the motoring articles I'd read in the newspapers, to grasp his full significance? I said in a low voice, 'It's not …it's not the gasket?'

He answered me frankly. 'Shall we say, it *might* possibly be the gasket. We need to perform numerous tests to find out. On the other hand, it might *not* be the gasket. At this stage, it would be unwise of me to give you a definite answer.'

'Mr Straker…'

I gulped. Yes! He must learn the truth, if only for my own good. It was a lapse, I tried consoling myself, no soul knew of it, certainly not Sandra, who quite justly would have despised me angrily.

'I must tell you something highly embarrassing,' I blurted. 'I'm deeply ashamed of it now, but I…er, exposed myself…to this complaint. I…omitted the antifreeze.'

How much better I felt at once!

'Now you mustn't entertain the slightest wickedness about it.' Mr Straker's voice was wise. 'To us garage-men, omitting the antifreeze is just another mechanical fault, we attach no more significance to it than that. My only object is getting your car fit for the road again as soon as possible, moral judgements have no place in the workshop. These days, omission of the antifreeze happens to some of the most respectable people, you'd be surprised, right here in Churchford.' I could not stop myself wondering who they might be. 'There's always a lot of it about this time of the year.'

I rubbed my palms together. 'I'm enormously grateful for your kindness and help, Mr Straker.'

'It's no more than I'm trained for, Doctor.'

'Of course, the whole matter's desperately worrying, but I *did* read in the papers how you can do wonderful things nowadays with spare parts. Fit an entirely new gasket, everything ticks over amazingly, drive back to your own garage, everyone pleased as punch, even if you do tend to blow up suddenly a couple of weeks later.'

'Yes, we've made many hopeful advances with the gasket.' Mr Straker expressed sober enthusiasm. 'Naturally, the press likes to sensationalize, and rather cruelly raises misplaced hopes. At least, we need no longer stand helplessly by and watch everything rust to bits, but of course much depends on how soon you come to us. I'm happy to say that the public is becoming better educated about this.'

'I hardly like mentioning it, as you're more of a friend than a technician, but it's going to cost a packet, I suppose? I'm not covered by any sort of scheme,' I added humbly.

'Would you discuss that with the garage receptionist?' he replied, a shade stiffly. 'She handles that part of it, and can supply you with my usual scale of fees. I think it might be advisable to perform an exploratory job now, Doctor.'

I gasped.

'Quite minor,' he reassured me. 'You'll be able to go home afterwards. Spanner!'

'Spanner.' I handed it to him.

'T-bar ratchet!'

'T-bar ratchet.'

'Feeler gauge!'

'Feeler gauge.'

'Swab! *Not there*, Doctor! Anyone would think you'd never had your hands in a bonnet before.' He concentrated on mysterious manipulations inside. 'Tell me, Doctor – don't you ever feel we'd be better off if the car had never been created?'

'It's a Mephistopheleian mix of convenience and curse. No longer just to keep your bum off the tarmac, but a mobile room of your own, ideal for all activities from confidential conferences to casual copulation. An instrument of aggression, cherished like a samurai's sword. An emblem of importance more ostentatious than the number of umbrellas over a Siamese nobleman. A badge of virility more flashy than a Tudor codpiece, an assurance of wealth more amusing than a bank statement, a print of personality more telling than a Rorschach inkblot. It's the most expensive toy in the world. It compels more fantasies than marijuana, more envy than vanished youth, more contempt than cowardice, more resentment than taxes, more offence than swearing in church and more impatience than paralysis. It's a slice of the household capital – or household debt – which men pride themselves on maintaining unblemished, in preference to their wives, and intact, rather than their daughters. It turns us all into potential criminals, it levels us more savagely than Communism. And as the Bard noticed, drink provokes the desire to drive but it takes away the performance. How can you concentrate on a tricky piece of work,' I broke off, 'with me rabbiting on like this?'

'If I *didn't* enjoy a chat on the job, then you should be worried. Oh, I know it's a crisis for you, Doctor. But to us it's routine, unless we're silenced by difficult complications. Get it? I'm ready to close,' he announced, briskly dabbing. 'Twelve-sided ring spanner!'

'Twelve-sided ring spanner.'

The bonnet snapped shut. 'Now I must go and scrub up.'

I detained him. 'But tell me…is there any hope?'

'Doctor, you're the man who can take the truth – it's got to go back to the maker.'

'Oh, well, I'm bloody sight better off than if I told *you* you were going back to yours.'

Mr Straker grinned. Though I am getting a little tired of our game.

2 NOVEMBER

Miss Fludde (local librarian with big tits) appeared at evening surgery. Tits apparently now no trouble, but wishes to know her significance in the universe. Am furious at patients presenting problems better directed to Professor Sir Freddie Ayer, Archbishop of Canterbury or *Any Questions?*

Replied, why worry? Adding, I thought neatly, travel through life as though on Inter-City, don't worry about the rails, sleepers and things underneath, make yourself as comfortable as feasible in the circumstances.

Miss Fludde reveals often frets over significance question, waking at night, between stamping library books, on loo, cannot believe cosmic forces have no relation whatever to her. Says asks colleagues, boyfriends, borough librarian, but are unhelpful, indeed do not seem to wish to know, consulted me because I highly intelligent and deeply sympathetic. I suspect sexual basis to inner turmoil, asking damfool questions like that probably turns men off faster than smelly armpits. Got rid of her with a bottle of Petrolagar, she fortunately being constipated as well.

4 NOVEMBER

Miss Fludde reappeared this evening, requesting I give her full course of psychoanalysis, in depth. Explained patiently that average NHS consultation statistically proved to last three minutes, so analysis would resemble quick-fire cross-talk act. Suggest group therapy, this favoured by NHS as economical, a sort of psychological package tour.

Miss Fludde seemed crestfallen, even tearful, so asked what on her mind, apart from the universe. She said she thought herself a mystic, had entertained St Teresa and Lillie Langtry in her bedsitter. Sceptical. Recalled heated arguments in golf club with the major over the Loch Ness Monster. I maintained the possibility of a prehistoric beast inhabiting an insignificant Scottish pond was *nil*, compared with human ability to see things not there, happening all the time. Human vision complex, not like Polaroid snaps, entire brain involved. Told major seeing not at all believing, quoted him French doctor-author Céline (got his books from Miss Fludde after snubbed at St Botolph's reunion by Trotskyite nut-doctor), 'Man sees only what he looks at, and looks only at what he already has in mind.' Major always incensed because he *saw* monster at Drummadrochit, though well known he could see it in Trafalgar Square, with Chinese Dragons and Donald Duck.

Miss Fludde's constipation relieved, but also had sinusitis, so could dismiss her with a decongestant.

5 NOVEMBER

Miss Fludde back at evening surgery (Guy Fawkes bangs, doubtless casualties). In state of unwonted excitement over colleague home that morning from year in California (UCLA) bearing news of local psychological cults. Luckily, have read these up. Esalin University on Big Sur coast is log cabins, mineral baths, nudity, sun-bathing, though all earnestly analysed *in extenso*. est (small e) cult, 250 all day in ballroom shouting, also known as 'no piss therapy' as none allowed to leave. Primal scream is $6,000 (in advance) to relieve horrors, humiliations, pain of infancy, till scream out, 'Daddy, Mommy, be nice, I hate you' (much like end English family tennis match). Psychiatrist Wilhelm Reich insisted that current obvious attack on world by Martians was repulsable by earthlings' mass erotic energy, but got two years inside. Also Transactional Analysis (games), Rolfing (anti-gravity), acupuncture, *tai chi*, Masters and Johnson's sensate focusing with skin lotions in love labs. Overt transference is straightforward how's-your-father by the sex therapist, should make Freud's ashes whirr in their urn. Plus Insight, which did miracles for Arianna Stassinopoulos.

Sketched these for Miss Fludde, explained mostly honest Yankee quackery, like Buffalo Lithia Water. Dissertate that psychiatrists of the 1980s as comparatively impotent as physicians of the 1920s. Freudian inspiration of removing mental symptoms with mere words always uphill task, even he failed totally with English governess in Vienna (Miss Lucy R) who was haunted by smell of burnt pudding.

Miss Fludde persisted wished to discover true self, enjoy real happiness. I quoted (librarian, therefore well read) doctor-playwright Chekhov, 'Peace and contentment do not lie outside a man, but within him.' Imparted that many people happy in jail and many dead miserable sunning on the beach at Benidorm, so feeling happy probably due to blood chemistry, like feeling hungry. Expanded (as she, too, highly intelligent) how sad, all people wish to fulfil themselves, but most must swim through life underwater. Only those like Liz Taylor, Robin Day and Sheik Yamani can water-ski across surface (I thought that rather neat, too). Thanked me, said I only person in Churchford she could confide secrets of soul to, much preferable to borough librarian. Her sinusitis improved but left red-tipped nose, got shot of her with ointment.

8 NOVEMBER

My first half-term visit to St Ursula's. Look into Head's study beside front door. Old Bill Hawesbury warned me (had briefed self on what entailed beforehand) always appear desperate to save life elsewhere, thus avoiding overdose of conversation.

'Good evening, Headmistress. Just paying my respects before going back to the surgery –'

'Ah, Doctor, come in. The annual physical examination of the entire senior school must leave you utterly whacked, but a glass of Cyprus sherry and you'll be a rose revived. Sit you down under the *monstera deliciosa* and regale yourself, the bottle's with the *TLS* in the Canterbury.'

Bill Hawesbury also warned about the Cyprus. Obediently took austere Habitat chair, presumably for delinquent girls.

'Too bad you hadn't a chance to watch the hockey, Doctor, so depressing the school being beaten by double figures, but of course the girls won't drink their milk these days, they're all more terrified of losing their figures than losing their virginity. Why, you've hardly poured yourself a thimbleful.'

'Cyprus sherry has an explosive effect on the breathalyzer, it's well known.'

'Let's have a chin-wag about the sort of things I tell the girls when I speak to them straight from the shoulder. What are *your* views on virginity, Doctor?'

'I regard it only as a gynaecological condition.'

'I blame all this premarital sex, what we used to call a dirty weekend, on Access and Barclaycard. I mean the idea behind them,' she amplified. 'Everyone wants to take the waiting out of wanting, in my young days the middle class thought anything smelling of hire-purchase rather vulgar, you never enjoyed the goods until you'd saved up for them, whether they were the bedroom suite or the bride.'

'I've noticed that people who make such a fuss about virginity are seldom those who possess it –'

'I had my sex education from my father the admiral,' Mrs Charrington revealed. 'I was ten at the time, he told me one morning, "Better make a good breakfast, I'm going to explain the facts of life," so I said, "Aye, aye, sir," we were having our summer hols on a farm and the bull was going to service the cows.'

'I've never found anyone despondent about losing their virginity, on the contrary –'

'So I finished my bacon and eggs and went into the farmyard with the admiral, I remember it was such a lovely day, and there was the bull, with its dander up, as you might say, but the cow took fright, you could hardly blame the poor thing, it was like being propositioned by the Cornish Riviera Express, the cow charged across the farmyard with the bull bellowing after it, right in the path of a tractor with a trailer of potatoes, which had to swerve and crashed through the greenhouses into the duckpond, the farmer tried to corner the bull with a pitchfork but it tossed him into the piggery and broke his leg, the farmer's wife who was feeding the poultry climbed a tree and the hens went screeching everywhere, then the bull chased the cow into the barn where the hands were brewing up their morning cuppa, it upset the Primus and the hay caught alight, the barn burnt to the ground and set the farmhouse roof ablaze, they had fire engines from three counties, I was terribly excited but my own wedding night seemed a bit of an anticlimax.'

'A booklet on these matters in simple, non-technical language is obtainable from the British Medical Association,' I informed her. 'Sixty-five p, they don't accept stamps.'

'Naturally, I warn the girls on the last day of term after prayers about the danger of getting Harry preggers. Though really they have no more excuse for it than for making themselves sick from over-eating, you doctors have so many little devices these days. When George and I were courting he had to keep buying rubber goods at the barbers, he had so many haircuts my father wondered why he had to go round looking like a German general. If you ask me, that's why all the young men then wore short hair, the Beatle-length fashion only came in with the pill.'

I countered this interesting suggestion with, 'I suppose the present passion for beards is only to show who's who in a unisex world?'

'Which brings me to something I despair of ridding St Ursula's of, no more than cockroaches and hanging participles. I mean crushes and pashes, which are now called Women's Liberation. Though it's just as bad among the staff, Cookery and Geography perform in an outrageously liberated way, right in the common room, of course I have to be dreadfully tactful, but Geography becomes perfectly unreasonable when I ask her not to smoke cigars and to use a pointer rather than a riding-crop at the blackboard. Personally, I'd like to give them a good hosing down in the yard, but as I can't see what any man could find in either of them, particularly Cookery, who looks like a rabbit in need of orthodontics, I suppose it's a case of any port in a storm, as the admiral used to say.'

'Homosexuality is a normal feature of childhood,' I pointed out. Decided Mrs Charrington a sensible woman, except over sherry. 'It's persistence into adult life represents a failure of emotional maturation—'

'Could you believe it, the fifth form actually sent me a round robin last summer demanding they use the swimming pool topless! I do wish they'd keep their minds on their O levels. I suppose its another sign of the times, in my young days a woman would no more think of baring her bos than my father of showing me he felt seasick, but nowadays titties are as commonplace as elbows.'

'It's been most interesting chatting to you—'

'But you can't toddle off yet, you've barely touched your sherry,' she reprimanded me. 'Of course, the whole business of health education has become so complicated, when I was a gel they told us to wear wool next to the skin and keep our legs crossed, and we seemed to thrive on it. All life's complicated, isn't it? I remember, on Saturday nights I'd get into my open MG and take George on a pub crawl, now if the police so much as get a whiff of shandygaff they treat you like a bank-robber. Quite ridiculous, my father could drive a battleship perfectly well when he was awash with pink gin.'

I leapt to my feet.

'What's the matter, Doctor?' she exclaimed.

Grabbed top pocket. 'My bleep. Emergency. I must rush.'

'But I didn't hear anything.'

'It's one of the new supersonic ones.'

'Whatever will they think of next? I hope we'll see you at the half-term concert on Saturday? I can certainly promise you a jolly evening and there'll be coffee with the entire staff afterwards.'

'I have rather a lot of gravely ill patients at the moment—'

'The fifth form are doing a send-up of *Camelot*, but by the time I've blue-pencilled the *double entendres* it'll only run two and a half minutes. Off you go, then, Doctor, on your merciful way. Can you imagine what Lulu Rossingham replied when Divinity asked in class who made her? "You mean originally or lately?" Really!'

14 NOVEMBER

Sandra and I to Sunday morning drinks at Chris' (in advertising). Arrive with trepidation and titillation, as Mrs Noakes and Mrs Blessington certain to be there. Not seen either since summer. Assume both still enamoured of me, things change slowly in Churchford society.

They appear overjoyed with my arrival, I give enigmatic smile, maybe just smug. Remembering last party (and Sandra only two topers away) converse in generalities, how number of shopping days to Christmas grows longer every year. Mrs Blessington purrs over Noilly Prat, 'You sexy one, you.'

Reply, amazing how Christmas has extended, remember when it meant a couple of days off, now lasts the best part of three weeks, from Friday before Christmas Eve to Tuesday after New Year's Day, no wonder national ruination stares one in the face.

Mrs Noakes says, 'Absolutely everyone's heard about it.'

Demand what.

'Why, you and that little girl in the public library,' clarifies Mrs Blessington.

Appalled.

'An absolutely *torrid* affair by all accounts,' murmurs Mrs Noakes.

Thunderstruck.

'She's terribly attractive, I gather,' suggests Mrs Blessington.

'Oh, makes Fiona Richmond look like Shirley Williams,' adds Mrs Noakes.

'Not yet eighteen,' amplifies Mrs Blessington.

'Not yet seventeen, *I* heard,' Mrs Noakes corrects her.

Grip brow. 'But this is a canard, a scandal, a slander, a barefaced fib!'

'*Come*, Doctor, own up,' Mrs Blessington invites gently. 'The girl who does my hair told me every single detail.'

'She lives next door to *your* voluptuous little girl,' Mrs Noakes informs me.

'You *have* made a hit, Doctor. Your girlfriend's telling everyone you're the most intelligent feller in Churchford.'

'Streets ahead of the borough librarian,' Mrs Noakes emphasizes.

Gulp gin and ton. 'I categorically deny every word.'

Both laugh. 'As the famous Mandy Rice-Davies said, "Well, he would, wouldn't he?" ' suggests Mrs Blessington.

'My relationship with Miss Fludde is strictly that of doctor and patient.'

'*Of course,*' observes Mrs Noakes, 'she called at your surgery three days running, Marjorie Palmer with the daily treatment for her toddler told me.'

'To be *psychoanalysed,*' Mrs Blessington reveals darkly. 'You never do anything like that to me on your couch, Doctor.'

'We're all dreadfully, *dreadfully* jealous,' Mrs Noakes points out.

Luckily, the Major appears with rerun of his operation (ribald). I stagger across lounge, instant vision GMC, obloquy, disgrace, ruin, GPs constant target of fantasies by unbalanced and constipated women. Impossible make party conversation, simply down gin and ton after gin and ton. Hope desperately the contumely confined to female gossips affected by hot air of hair-dryers, but Chris slaps me on back when leaving, saying, 'I must read more books, Doc, widens the experience, eh, nudge nudge, wink wink, nuf said, lucky sod.' Sandra drives home, decide not worth mentioning it to her. Sat silently, explaining many professional worries on mind, she says you're pissed as usual.

All Sunday ruined. Couldn't sleep. Woke Sandra round 2 a.m. to confide this horrifying accusation, she said, really, would I remind her to order more dehydrated tripe for the dog in the morning.

15 NOVEMBER

Worse.

Dropped into golf club after evening surgery, found Arthur Crevin, editor of *Churchford Echo*, obese and loudmouthed, plays in comic T-shirt, should never have been elected, but useful for perpetuating medal winners, hole-in-one, etc. Greeted me loudly across crowded bar, 'Hello, you randy old bastard, having it off like a rattlesnake with the Lolita of the library, eh?'

Exclaimed aghast, 'Not a word of truth. Mrs Noakes and Mrs Blessington made it all up in the hairdresser's.'

'Come off it, Doctor, the little lovely sent a vivid account to the *Echo* office. I must say, we all enjoyed reading it, right down to the tea lady and doorman.'

Protested strongly, 'Do you imagine for one moment I am a man likely to behave thus?'

Arthur Crevin guffawed. 'Wish I'd half the chance myself, she sent along her photos. Don't worry, we won't publish anything,' he continued with grating condescension. 'Luckily for you, our libel laws restrict free speech.'

Now cynosure all eyes. Horribly embarrassing, particularly as the major etc. indulged in pathetic schoolboy banter. Continue assert innocence, all vile calumny, sickening feeling my dear friends don't believe me for one moment, atrocious how mankind unfailingly thinks the worst of its fellows, applies own low standards, or perhaps just dead envious. Windrush the pathologist at the General appears in the bar with his medical-student sense of humour, leave.

Outside, suspect behind every bush Nigel Dempster, William Hickey, the man from *Private Eye*. God! Can see now labelled for life in *Eye* 'The Dirty Doctor', sneering story in smudgy print, past peccadilloes inflated, probably theatre sister's knicker elastic, made to appear like those GPs in trouble (generally in Lancashire, for some reason) examining girls' tits for tonsillitis. Useless suing for libel, they organize 'Gordonballs Fund', anyway look bigger prune in court explaining matters to fish-eyed barrister who had probably got to hear of Mrs Blessington's bandage.

16 NOVEMBER

Courageously, perhaps foolhardily, entered library to confront Miss Fludde, appeal to better nature, deny all, threaten proceedings, etc. She not there. Entire staff stare as though I Rex Harrison playing Jack the Ripper. Borough librarian opens office door, groans, 'Oh, no!' loudly, shuts it. Hide in Fiction I – P, grab armful, pretend just came to refresh mind, stare hard at upper shelves when leaving not to notice girl who unable to stamp flyleaves from suppressed giggles. Go home, find books dreadfully dull, Henry James (Complete Works), Ouida's *Two Little Wooden Shoes* and Pilnyak's *The Volga Falls to the Caspian Sea*.

26 NOVEMBER

Amazed as Mrs Shakespear bursts into morning surgery. She waves waiting-room copy of this week's *Woman's Glory*. Points quiveringly to big story lavishly illustrated in colour, 'Lovely Doctor' by Marie-Anne Fludde, 'exciting new writer, read this tale vibrant with the passion of a librarian for *elderly* GP'. Furious. Tell Mrs Shakespear burn it in back yard, she says of course not, wants to read it.

Luckily, Adrian (publisher) morning patient, angrily tell him whole story, ask shall I sue her for libel? He says far from it, demand cut into her royalties, haven't I heard? M-A Fludde hottest property since Erica Jong, even Agatha Christie, her coming *Sex and the Stethoscope* already buzzed in the trade as selling millions, big tits of course great literary asset, she gone to California to save tax and sort herself out.

30 NOVEMBER

Have rude letter from borough librarian, demanding payment of £8 fine for non-return of *The Magic Mountain* since last February.

DECEMBER

1 DECEMBER

Called out to emergency at St Ursula's. Treat case, leave instructions with Matron, retire towards car on speedy tiptoe, like Fred Astaire routine.

'Why, Doctor! Anyone would think you were trying to sneak past my study door. Little Lulu Rossingham's only a sprained kneecap, I hope. Though she's such a super goalie, I wouldn't jib at her playing in a plaster cast. Come and refresh yourself with a draught of Cyprus and a Garibaldi, what we used to call squashed-fly bikkies, sit down next to the escritoire, the bottle's behind the tadpoles.'

'I'll just take the biscuit, thanks, Headmistress. My patients wouldn't care to be engulfed by the heady, exotic fumes of Famagusta.'

'I'm glad I caught you this morning, I've a few minutes before lunch and wanted a natter about something I confiscated from the fifth form. Shift over a bit, and I'll spring open the secret compartment, the escritoire belonged to my maiden aunt Judy – when she croaked, we found it full of letters burning with passion, in fact utterly obscene, addressed to her from a clergyman in Norwich, my father the admiral decided she'd written them all herself, she'd never excite any man enough even to give up his seat to her on the Tube.'

Agreed feelingly, 'Quite likely. Fantasywise, sex makes Disneyland look like Birmingham.'

Had Mrs Charrington heard of Miss Fludde? Might I be expelled from St Ursula's?

'The cache,' explained Mrs Charrington, sliding aside the false inkwells, 'now contains this dog-eared – indeed, tattered – paperback by one Miss Wendy Leigh, *What Makes a Woman Good in Bed*, though as far as my girls are concerned, it's not chattering after lights-out. Pretty hot stuff, I warn you.' She handed it over. 'Even if it does read like the combination of a Guides' cookery course and an army instruction manual on basic infantry tactics. Personally, I can't see the need for such books, once you've learned to ride a bike you can surely mount whenever you feel like it, and if you want to steer with your feet on the handlebars you don't get there any quicker.'

'Yes, Headmistress, as Thoreau really said, the mass of men live lives of quiet copulation. And as Nancy Mitford – who wrote about sex as sensibly as Jane Austen – remarked of pre-Freudian days, it was then an act of limited importance, resembling eating, drinking and praying, not one of mystical awe. You'd be amazed at the number of people who fret terribly they haven't reached the sexual touchlines, they might be missing some wonderful physical experience which probably doesn't exist, like levitation.'

'It seems from these pages that a girl now loses a man's respect if she *doesn't* go to bed with him, instead of vice versa, the first man I rebuffed certainly respected me, though admittedly I knocked out a couple of his front teeth. All those peculiar positions, anyone would imagine they awarded couples points for dressage, I can't see it makes much difference if you blow your nose standing up or lying down.'

I observed, flicking over the text (no pictures), 'The pleasure may be fleeting and the posture ridiculous, but the curiosity is endless.'

'And a little learning is a dangerous thing. Middle-School Maths – rather drippy, weaves her own clothes, you'd never have expected it of her – confided that on honeymoon her husband fell out of bed and broke a leg, they were staying B and B in remote Scotland, where they take a rather serious view of such things, particularly at three in the morning, but she was better off than one of my father's gunnery officers, who had to have the Portsmouth fire brigade called out with axes. These manuals would make handy packs with Dr Spock, wouldn't they? Funny how people no longer trust themselves doing what comes naturally like Annie Oakley. I seem to have confiscated dozens of them in my time – naturally, I have to read them to know the girls' minds, though I suppose these things can't help being as identical as geometry textbooks. I found Lulu Rossingham with this companion volume in the sicker this morning, *What Makes a Man Good in Bed*, I read it during bun-break, I must say the ladies interviewed seem perfectionists, though some of the men mentioned – Richard Burton, Andy Warhol, Prince Egon von Furstenberg and the like, don't have to worry about overstraining their backs digging the garden as well.'

She replaced her Index Librorum Prohibitorum. 'Can *you* tell in any marriage, Doctor,' she enquired, 'if the husband's playing away fixtures?'

'From the kitchen. The luxury of the fittings is directly proportional to the guilt over the mistresses.'

'These volumes probably cause as much giggling as titillation.' She clicked back the panel which sealed the crypt of her aunt's love-life. 'Though a lot of my girls behave like teenage Cleopatras, they're more frightened of sex than the dentist. They'll all end up as happily humdrum housewives, thank Heaven, even my other maiden aunt Hilda got married pushing fifty, she was dreadfully hesitant, but my father told her better copulate than never. Must you go, Doctor? Take a couple of chocolate Viennas to munch on your way, your patients can't possibly object to the crumbs.'

5 DECEMBER

Sunday. Andy appeared unexpectedly in Alfa. Cock-a-hoop as won St Botolph's houseman gold medal, starting next month coveted registrar's job with Sir Rollo, then year's surgical scholarship fixed at Massachusetts General, Boston. Clearly, he not such a dimwit as I always imagined. Strange when your children become your professional colleagues. Stranger, when your professional superiors. Console self it's all genetic. To keep Andy in place, quote Queen Elizabeth I's surgeon, John Woodall, 'It is no small presumption to dismember the image of God.' He laughs, 'To most surgeons, Dad, they and God make a nice pair.'

6 DECEMBER

Checking Christmas card list this evening, when (Dr) Toby Hatchett phones to say old pal Fred Findhorn (GP at Maidencester) just died, memorial service at St Botolph's chapel end of month. Cross him off list.

20 DECEMBER

To St Ursula's, all paper-chains and fun.

'Jolly D of you, Doctor, to grace the girls' end-of-term carol service.' Felt had as little alternative as Queen avoiding Trooping the Colour. 'After that rendition of "Away in a Manger" I expect you want to wet your whistle.' Mrs Charrington propelled me firmly into study.

'Sit you down beside Oliver Cromwell's bust and regale yourself with a glass of Cyprus, the bottle's behind the A J P Taylor. With hindsight, I must say it was a mistake letting the fifth read the lesson on the nativity, Lulu Rossingham smacking her lips over being great with child and so on, the fifth have a hairspring snigger-trigger for anything remotely connected with sex, the earthier bits of the sixteenth century are quite impossible to teach, and English simply had to abandon *Romeo and Juliet* when they started interpreting the balcony scene like an X movie. I say, that's a mean ration, 'tis Christmas, season of wassail and brimming bumpers.'

'I always think, Headmistress, that Cyprus sherry tastes best in small quantities.'

'I hope you noticed Middle-School Maths this evening, Doctor?' She shot a sharp glance from her armchair. 'The one in the homespun dress, crocheted bandeau and flip-flops.'

Reflected, 'She seemed to let herself go a bit with "Hark! the Herald Angels Sing…".'

'And?'

Shrugged.

'Preggers,' Mrs Charrington pronounced. 'Perfectly inconsiderate of her, she's going to pup right in the middle of O levels, and our trigonometry's weak enough as it is. Maths has a disgustingly primitive

RICHARD GORDON

approach to childbearing, she'd be happiest having it in the corner of a paddy field like the Chinese.'

Murmured, 'It's much safer for both, having a baby in hospital. But lots of mothers feel outraged at overturning their domestic arrangements, you might have suggested enjoying family Christmas dinner in the works canteen.'

'Middle-School Maths caused endless trouble with her last one, parading the poor little thing up and down the High Street and outing her titties to feed it in public, to protest against the supermarkets and post office and hamburger bars not providing facilities for Nature's needs, quite ridiculous when they don't even provide parking, and anyway she said in Italy mothers do it absolutely everywhere except the Vatican, but of course Italians are only peasants with Fiats. Naturally, the managers complained that their male customers objected, though I understand in the sleazy streets of London men pay good money to see such things. I suppose it's the difference between a beautiful vista of inactive volcanoes and a couple of them erupting under your nose. She got arrested in the public library because of the notice about no eating and drinking, but at the police station they let her do it in a cell.'

'I always tell my maternity cases the breast is a wonderful bargain for pre-packed baby food, especially at today's prices. No messing about with measures and bottles, apply to baby and forget it, as convenient as shake-and-bake cake mix.'

'Pregnancy isn't what it was, like everything else,' Mrs Charrington lamented, rising to sprinkle some ants' eggs into the goldfish beside the *fuchsia magellanica*. 'It's commercialized quite as callously as Christmas, people seem as mad on accessories for their babies as for their cars, those mothers' shops sell the equivalent of the little square cushions and the dogs with eyes that light up you get from the garage. There's no mystery left, with them letting in the husbands to watch the fireworks, my father the admiral would no more have observed my mother in action than taken his morning bath in the WRNS' ablutions.'

'It's the progressive idea, childbirth to become family fun like home movies.'

156

'I decided to allow George to watch me have our little Rodney, though usually he's not in the slightest interested in strenuous physical activities, I mean nothing on earth would get him to watch sports day. When the nurse in the maternity hospital dressed him up, he could have passed as a part-time brain surgeon. But you know George is no giant, in fact you could lose him among the junior school, his hat flopped over his eyes like the ones from the Christmas crackers, and with the mask across his nose he saw less than a medieval knight with his ventail clamped against his bevore and gorget. He wasn't too concerned about *that*, with the grunts and groans and the clank of cutlery in his ears once at the seat of action, as it were, he felt he might have been overconfident and would measure his length on the terrazzo, like the time he went to a bullfight in Malaga. When the nurse pressed the child into George's arms he managed to make the right sort of baby noises, but there was a dreadful scream and the mother shouted quite vulgarly who's that little bugger, my husband's driving a lorry to Newcastle. For some reason she wanted George run in for indecent exposure. I had to rise from my childbed in the next door labour room with Rodney in my arms and sort it all out. Have a shortbread with your sherry, they're petticoat-tail.'

'Headmistress, there's something I've been itching to ask you all term.'

'Fire away.'

'Why did you choose me for St Ursula's?'

'Apart from your professional skills, Doctor, I always find you so interesting to talk to. Won't you join the staff in a bit of supper? The cook's *macaroni au gratin* is indeed her *tour de force*. Oh, what a pity, you've hundreds of patients to see and it's getting on for Christmas. I'd have liked you to run an eye over Divinity, I've a nasty feeling she's going to let me down over O levels, too.'

25 DECEMBER

Peace on Earth. Goodwill to All Men, who for once are most considerately not falling ill. Enjoying Scotch, home-made cake, soap, herbal sachets, marmalade, secateurs, tissues, satsumas, oven cloth, toothpaste-tube squeezer, bars chocolate, hand mirror with CHEER UP! inscribed across it.

RICHARD GORDON

All presents from patients despite National Health Service costing every
man, woman and child of them £240 a year (in 1949, £8.75 each a year).
Reflected, the doctor still part of everybody's family, despite medicine
becoming highly scientific activity, as effectively performed by Drs Barty-
Howells and Windrush at the General. Remembered Thomas Mann called
medicine 'That subdivision of the humanities', also remembered cannot
trace *The Magic Mountain*, God knows what borough librarian will sting me.

31 DECEMBER

Gloomy, drizzly day. Just before lunchtime, in the Goat and Compasses
opposite St Botolph's Hospital.

'Morning dear! Large single malt, no water and certainly no ice – good
God, Mick,' I exclaimed, 'you here already? You must hold the sprint
record from the hospital chapel to the Goat. These memorial services *do*
leave a need for urgent pharmacological treatment, don't they? And the
same again for my friend,' I addressed the redhead with the lurex T-shirt
tight across her knockers.

'I thought the chaplain operated smoothly and Sir Rollo's address hit
just the note,' (Dr) Mick O'Fawl asserted. 'All about poor old Fred
Findhorn's selfless devotion to his patients, skirting round him being
struck off for three years, though the woman made him an excellent
second wife. Cheers, Richard.'

'Cheers. Poor old Fred!'

'Seems only yesterday Fred and I were standing here when the blitz
demolished out-patients' but only killed the matron's cat.' Mick was
senior to me. 'These sort of outings jolt you, realizing how long ago the
War was.'

I nodded. 'Do you know, my son Andy actually asked me the other
night, Who was Stanley Baldwin? As though he was Mr Gladstone.'

'Surely *everyone* knows the PM whose lips were sealed and overlooked
rearmament?' Mick frowned. 'Why, our children will be muddling Adolf
and Musso next.'

'Then my daughter Jilly says, Stanley Baldwin's Peter Barkworth, like
Winston Churchill's Robert Hardy and Edward VII's Timothy West and

Edward VIII's Edward Fox. Do you realize, Orwell's nightmare of rewriting history is already here? To the younger generation, the past is what happens tonight on TV.'

'When I tell my kids about medicine during the War – could we both have the same again, please – ?'

'Christ, you two haven't wasted any time.' (Dr) Dave Devonport-Campbell, appeared through the door marked TAPROOM, slapping Mick on the back. 'Make that three.'

'My kids just say,' Mick continued, "Dad, the war is as far from us now as hansom cabs and Queen Victoria were from you then." They're absolutely right, work it out. Sobering thought.'

'Medicine was far less comfortable before these days of tranquillizers and Terramycin,' Dave reflected. 'We seemed to treat everything with scalding poultices or turpentine enemas.'

'We'll be needing the repeat, when you're free,' I instructed the barmaid. 'A memorial service is only a man's friends getting pissed in black ties. I remember vividly those old times when the surgeons behaved like King Kong with fleas, and ward sisters made the Ride of the Valkyries look like showjumping at Hickstead, but I can't remember my patients' names. That's diagnostic of senility?'

'Or alcoholism,' Mick suggested.

'In your case, both combined,' said Dave.

'Well, as the creator of Rumpole of the Bailey said so wisely,' I recalled, '"No pleasure is worth giving up for the sake of an extra three years in a geriatric home in Weston-super-Mare." Cheers!'

'And post-mortem cheers to poor old Fred,' Mick added.

'Splendid fellow, wasn't he?' observed Dave. 'Well, a bit of a bastard really, I suppose.'

'Through Fred I failed my medical clinical,' Mick asserted. 'He'd just come out, and tipped me that the examiner rather liked you to demonstrate – on the first patient to the left – that the lung had collapsed and been replaced with air, by using the coin test.'

'The old coin test!' cried Dave nostalgically. 'Tapping them on the patient's chest. The bell of anvil sound! The *bruit d'airain!* Nowadays, you'd use nothing more romantic than a computer printout. They don't make symptoms and signs like that any more.'

'So I produced two coins – those vast half-crowns – the patient immediately pocketed them and said, "Ta, Guv, I've got what they call a pneumothorax." The examiner overheard and chucked me out. I think Fred himself had got away with it.'

'What did Fred die of?' enquired Dave.

'Pulmonary embolism complicating emphysema,' I told him.

'Excuse me, Richard, but pulmonary embolism is *never* a complication of emphysema,' said Mick.

'I beg your pardon. Any first-year student would tell you that pulmonary embolism is the commonest complication of emphysema.'

'Rubbish. You're not thinking of asthma.'

'*I am not!* You're telling me I'm a medical ignoramus?'

'Well, everyone said you only got qualified because you were having it off with the Dean's daughter.'

'*What?* That bag? You are suggesting, O'Fawl, that I was a young man of *such poor taste* I'd have chucked a brick through a Gainsborough.'

'What's the odds? She's got eight grandchildren now. Same again?'

'Why, here's Ian!' exclaimed Dave, as the door swung open. 'We're on the single malt. What did Fred die of?'

'He died of Henoch-Schönlein purpura.'

'That's impossible, Ian,' I objected.

'Why?'

'Fred was such an incompetent doctor he'd never have heard of it. And here's Alfie! What did Fred die of?'

'Of a Saturday.'

'God, that's funny!' I chortled. '*Bloody* funny!'

'We're all getting old,' grumbled Mick.

'Not a bit,' Dave objected. 'You only get old if you forget to close your zip when you have a pee.'

'You only get *really* old,' Alfie corrected him, 'if you forget to open your zip when you have a pee.'

'Christ, that's bloody, *bloody* funny!' I roared. 'Same again, all round? Mick, Dave, Ian, Alfie, drink up! Here's to the next St Botolph's memorial service, the five of us *must* meet afterwards in the Goat and Compasses…well…perhaps…maybe the four of us?'

We stared at each other.

I gave a long sigh. 'Ho-hummmmm! Well… Cheers!'

What other way is there to look at life?

RICHARD GORDON

DOCTOR IN THE HOUSE

Richard Gordon's acceptance into St Swithin's medical school came as no surprise to anyone, least of all him – after all, he had been to public school, played first XV rugby, and his father was, let's face it, 'a St Swithin's man'. Surely he was set for life. It was rather a shock then to discover that, once there, he would actually have to work, and quite hard. Fortunately for Richard Gordon, life proved not to be all dissection and textbooks after all… This hilarious hospital comedy is perfect reading for anyone who's ever wondered exactly what medical students get up to in their training. Just don't read it on your way to the doctor's!

'Uproarious, extremely iconoclastic' – *Evening News*
'A delightful book' – *Sunday Times*

DOCTOR AT SEA

Richard Gordon's life was moving rapidly towards middle-aged lethargy – or so he felt. Employed as an assistant in general practice – the medical equivalent of a poor curate – and having been 'persuaded' that marriage is as much an obligation for a young doctor as celibacy for a priest, Richard sees the rest of his life stretching before him. Losing his nerve, and desperately in need of an antidote, he instead signs on with the Fathom Steamboat Company. What follows is a hilarious tale of nautical diseases and assorted misadventures at sea. Yet he also becomes embroiled in a mystery – what is in the Captain's stomach remedy? And more to the point, what on earth happened to the previous doctor?

'Sheer unadulterated fun' – *Star*

Richard Gordon

Doctor at Large

Dr Richard Gordon's first job after qualifying takes him to St Swithin's where he is enrolled as Junior Casualty House Surgeon. However, some rather unfortunate incidents with Mr Justice Hopwood, as well as one of his patients inexplicably coughing up nuts and bolts, mean that promotion passes him by – and goes instead to Bingham, his odious rival. After a series of disastrous interviews, Gordon cuts his losses and visits a medical employment agency. To his disappointment, all the best jobs have already been snapped up, but he could always turn to general practice…

Great Medical Disasters

Man's activities have been tainted by disaster ever since the serpent first approached Eve in the garden. And the world of medicine is no exception. In this outrageous and strangely informative book, Richard Gordon explores some of history's more bizarre medical disasters. He creates a catalogue of mishaps including anthrax bombs on Gruinard Island, destroying mosquitoes in Panama, and Mary the cook who, in 1904, inadvertently spread typhoid across New York State. As the Bible so rightly says, 'He that sinneth before his maker, let him fall into the hands of the physician.'

Richard Gordon

The Private Life of Jack The Ripper

In this remarkably shrewd and witty novel, Victorian London is brought to life with a compelling authority. Richard Gordon wonderfully conveys the boisterous, often lusty panorama of life for the very poor – hard, menial work; violence; prostitution; disease. *The Private Life of Jack The Ripper* is a masterly evocation of the practice of medicine in 1888 – the year of Jack the Ripper. It is also a dark and disturbing medical mystery. Why were his victims so silent? And why was there so little blood?

'…horribly entertaining…excitement and suspense buttressed with authentic period atmosphere' – *The Daily Telegraph*

The Invisible Victory

Jim Elgar is a young chemist struggling to find work in nineteen-thirties' Britain. He moves instead to the scientific world in Germany and finds himself perfectly placed to undertake top-secret work for the British war effort. His ensuing role in counter-espionage takes him on a high-speed spy-chase through Europe, only just ahead of the invading Nazis. *The Invisible Victory* is the story of cut-throat medical research and life-saving discoveries in the face of wide-scale suffering and death.

TITLES BY RICHARD GORDON AVAILABLE DIRECT
FROM HOUSE OF STRATUS

Quantity		£	$(US)	$(CAN)	€
	THE CAPTAIN'S TABLE	6.99	11.50	15.99	11.50
	DOCTOR AND SON	6.99	11.50	15.99	11.50
	DOCTOR AT LARGE	6.99	11.50	15.99	11.50
	DOCTOR AT SEA	6.99	11.50	15.99	11.50
	DOCTOR IN CLOVER	6.99	11.50	15.99	11.50
	DOCTOR IN LOVE	6.99	11.50	15.99	11.50
	DOCTOR IN THE HOUSE	6.99	11.50	15.99	11.50
	DOCTOR IN THE NEST	6.99	11.50	15.99	11.50
	DOCTOR IN THE NUDE	6.99	11.50	15.99	11.50
	DOCTOR IN THE SOUP	6.99	11.50	15.99	11.50
	DOCTOR IN THE SWIM	6.99	11.50	15.99	11.50
	DOCTOR ON THE BALL	6.99	11.50	15.99	11.50
	DOCTOR ON THE BOIL	6.99	11.50	15.99	11.50
	DOCTOR ON THE BRAIN	6.99	11.50	15.99	11.50
	DOCTOR ON THE JOB	6.99	11.50	15.99	11.50
	DOCTOR ON TOAST	6.99	11.50	15.99	11.50
	DOCTORS' DAUGHTERS	6.99	11.50	15.99	11.50
	THE FACEMAKER	6.99	11.50	15.99	11.50
	GOOD NEIGHBOURS	6.99	11.50	15.99	11.50

ALL HOUSE OF STRATUS BOOKS ARE AVAILABLE FROM GOOD BOOKSHOPS OR
DIRECT FROM THE PUBLISHER:

Internet: **www.houseofstratus.com** including author interviews, reviews, features.

Email: **sales@houseofstratus.com** please quote author, title and credit card details.

TITLES BY RICHARD GORDON AVAILABLE DIRECT
FROM HOUSE OF STRATUS

Quantity		£	$(US)	$(CAN)	€
	GREAT MEDICAL DISASTERS	6.99	11.50	15.99	11.50
	GREAT MEDICAL MYSTERIES	6.99	11.50	15.99	11.50
	HAPPY FAMILIES	6.99	11.50	15.99	11.50
	INVISIBLE VICTORY	6.99	11.50	15.99	11.50
	LOVE AND SIR LANCELOT	6.99	11.50	15.99	11.50
	NUTS IN MAY	6.99	11.50	15.99	11.50
	THE SUMMER OF SIR LANCELOT	6.99	11.50	15.99	11.50
	SURGEON AT ARMS	6.99	11.50	15.99	11.50
	THE PRIVATE LIFE OF DR CRIPPEN	6.99	11.50	15.99	11.50
	THE PRIVATE LIFE OF FLORENCE NIGHTINGALE	6.99	11.50	15.99	11.50
	THE PRIVATE LIFE OF JACK THE RIPPER	6.99	11.50	15.99	11.50

ALL HOUSE OF STRATUS BOOKS ARE AVAILABLE FROM GOOD BOOKSHOPS OR
DIRECT FROM THE PUBLISHER:

Hotline: UK ONLY: **0800 169 1780**, please quote author, title and credit card details.
INTERNATIONAL: **+44 (0) 20 7494 6400**, please quote author, title and
credit card details.

Send to: **House of Stratus Sales Department**
24c Old Burlington Street
London
W1X 1RL
UK

Please allow for postage costs charged per order plus an amount per book as set out in the tables below:

	£(Sterling)	$(US)	$(CAN)	€(Euros)
Cost per order				
UK	2.00	3.00	4.50	3.30
Europe	3.00	4.50	6.75	5.00
North America	3.00	4.50	6.75	5.00
Rest of World	3.00	4.50	6.75	5.00
Additional cost per book				
UK	0.50	0.75	1.15	0.85
Europe	1.00	1.50	2.30	1.70
North America	2.00	3.00	4.60	3.40
Rest of World	2.50	3.75	5.75	4.25

PLEASE SEND CHEQUE, POSTAL ORDER (STERLING ONLY), EUROCHEQUE, OR INTERNATIONAL MONEY ORDER (PLEASE CIRCLE METHOD OF PAYMENT YOU WISH TO USE)
MAKE PAYABLE TO: STRATUS HOLDINGS plc

Cost of book(s): —————————— Example: 3 x books at £6.99 each: £20.97

Cost of order: —————————— Example: £2.00 (Delivery to UK address)

Additional cost per book: —————— Example: 3 x £0.50: £1.50

Order total including postage: ———— Example: £24.47

Please tick currency you wish to use and add total amount of order:

☐ £ (Sterling)   ☐ $ (US)   ☐ $ (CAN)   ☐ € (EUROS)

VISA, MASTERCARD, SWITCH, AMEX, SOLO, JCB:

☐ ☐ ☐ ☐ ☐ ☐ ☐ ☐ ☐ ☐ ☐ ☐ ☐ ☐ ☐ ☐ ☐ ☐ ☐

Issue number (Switch only):

☐ ☐ ☐

Start Date: **Expiry Date:**

☐☐ / ☐☐   ☐☐ / ☐☐

Signature: ————————————

NAME: —————————————————————

ADDRESS: —————————————————————

—————————————————————

POSTCODE: ——————————

Please allow 28 days for delivery.

Prices subject to change without notice.
Please tick box if you do not wish to receive any additional information. ☐

House of Stratus publishes many other titles in this genre; please check our website (**www.houseofstratus.com**) for more details.